TEEN
REF
A GOOD "NO CALL"

TEEN REF

A GOOD "NO CALL"

PHIL STRUZZIERO

NEW YORK

NASHVILLE • MELBOURNE • VANCOUVER

TEEN REF
A Good "No Call"

Published in New York, New York, by Morgan James Publishing in partnership with Difference Press. Morgan James is a trademark of Morgan James, LLC. www.MorganJamesPublishing.com

The Morgan James Speakers Group can bring authors to your live event. For more information or to book an event visit The Morgan James Speakers Group at www.TheMorganJamesSpeakers Group.com.

ISBN 9781683505716 paperback
ISBN 9781683505723 eBook
Library of Congress Control Number: 2017907089

Cover Design by:
Megan Whitney
megan@creativeninjadesigns.com

Interior Design by:
Chris Treccani
www.3dogcreative.net

In an effort to support local communities, raise awareness and funds, Morgan James Publishing donates a percentage of all book sales for the life of each book to Habitat for Humanity Peninsula and Greater Williamsburg.

Get involved today! Visit
www.MorganJamesBuilds.com

For Kate, Caroline, and Libby

TABLE OF CONTENTS

Chapter 1

TEAM LEADER

All the girls want you, and all of the boys want to be you, thought Drew Hennings as he walked into the cafeteria at Hingham Middle School. Drew was fourteen, but he looked more like the new Spanish teacher working lunch duty than he did like his classmates. He was almost six feet tall. He had short brown hair and hazel eyes. Drew wore his black game jersey with red numbers; the team only wore black for big games. This was *the* big game, a Super Bowl game against archrival Duxbury. Drew was number 10, just like his Dad wore when he played wide receiver at Brown University. Drew's game jersey looked good, it smelled good, and Drew loved how he felt when he wore it. One of the cheerleaders liked how he looked in it too. When he walked by their table, she said, "Hey, Drew!"

Drew smiled as he walked by, *She's not as cute as Callie Walker,* he thought. It was pizza day at school, and Drew had bought pizza every Friday since he was in Kindergarten. The middle school had been built three years ago, and the cafeteria looked more like it belonged to Wheaton College than to a middle school in the Boston suburbs. There were floor to ceiling windows on three sides of the room. Drew walked slowly to his place at the table with the rest of the eighth grade football team. They sat against the window halfway between the entrance and the exit. They could see everybody, and everybody could see them. If it was a nice day and their teachers were in a good mood, then the boys could sneak out onto the new grass and throw the ball around.

Drew took his place in the center of the table and put his tray down. His best friend, Scott Myers, sat on his right. Scott was the starting left tackle. He had blond hair, a round face, and a formidable upper body. His cheeks were almost always red, but today he looked pale.

Drew ate half a slice of pizza in one bite and said, "What's wrong with you?"

"Trying to make weight," said Scott. He had a salad and a bottle of water in front of him.

"So you can't eat one of these?" teased Brendan Foster, the tailback, as he waved a golden cupcake with chocolate frosting in Scott's face. Scott did not look up.

"Knock it off, Foster!" said Drew.

"Sorry, Drew," said Brendan.

Drew stared at him.

"Sorry, Scott," said Brendan.

"The 170 pound weight limit is ridiculous," Drew said.

"Easy for you to say. You're five pounds under," said Scott.

Drew had planned to eat the two slices on his plate, jump back into line, and buy two more. *Better wait until I get home,* he thought.

"Last one, Scotty Boy," said Drew. "After we win on Sunday, I'll hand the trophy over to you and run to the snack shack. I'll buy you one of everything."

"It's gonna be awesome," said Scott.

"And just think: there's no weight limit in high school football. Hang in for two more days, and you'll never have to go through this again," Drew said.

Following Drew's lead, everyone at the table encouraged Scott.

"I heard that the Head Coach from Thayer Academy might come down to watch the game," said Troy Callahan, a receiver and Drew's favorite target.

"Who cares?" said Drew. "No one from their team ever gets scholarship offers from Division One schools. They all play at Division Three schools like Tufts or Wesleyan or Mass. Maritime."

"Thayer is more of a hockey school," said Scott.

Callie likes some freshman at Hingham High who plays on the JV hockey team. Drew looked over at Callie and took a deep breath. He caught himself. *Get a grip, kid.* Drew glanced at his friends, and they were trying not to laugh. *Busted,* thought Drew. He looked back at them and shrugged. *I wonder if I can change her mind?* he thought.

"Do you think that the Milton Academy Coach will be at the game?" asked Scott.

"He'll be there," said Drew.

"How do you know?" asked Brendan.

Drew chugged his sports drink. He slammed the empty bottle down on the table, and he said, "Because he told me on the phone last night!"

"Ohhh!" said the boys.

Drew continued, "He talked to me and my dad for like twenty minutes. He kept talking about how their quarterback signed with Yale, and Yale finally beat Harvard in The Game."

"Cool," said Troy.

"Yeah," Drew replied. "But Milton only plays eight games, and I couldn't play with all of you guys."

"What about Boston College High School?" asked Brendan.

"Their Coach will be at the game too. I talked to him last week," said Drew.

"Wait a second," said Scott. "You're not even Catholic!"

"I told him that, but he didn't seem to mind," said Drew.

"They're good," said Troy. "Don't they send a lot of guys to Boston College?"

"They usually do, but not this year," replied Drew. "My dad and I looked it up. They had six seniors commit to play college football, but none of them received offers from Division One schools."

"Really?" said Troy.

"Yup," said Drew. "They only won six games this year. Anyway, there's no way I'm going to an all boys' school." Drew looked at the cheerleaders' table again. His teammates followed his lead.

"Are you looking at Callie again?" asked Troy.

"Yeah," said Drew.

"Forget it, Drew," said Scott. "I heard that she's going out with some freshman hockey player."

"Things change," said Drew. *Come on. Look over here,* thought Drew. Callie was talking with her teammates. She wore her long, dark hair in a high pony tail tied with red ribbon. The ribbon had little, white H's on it. Drew was looking at the curls at the ends of her pony tail when he suddenly realized that she was looking directly at him. Drew smiled, and Callie giggled and kept talking to her friends. *Is she laughing at me?* thought Drew.

"Real smooth, Romeo," said Scott.

Troy tried to help Drew by changing the subject, "So what plays do you think Coach is going to call on Sunday night?"

"Slot Right 95 Sprint Pass," said Drew.

"Troy's touchdown catch on that play last week against Marshfield was absolutely savage!" said Brendan.

"It was," said Drew. "But you were open too, B. Sorry about that."

"Do you hear me complaining? We're in the Super Bowl, baby!" Brendan said, and he gave Drew a high five.

Slot Right 95 Sprint Pass had three options, and no team that had played Hingham could stop all three.

"First, I line up split to the right," said Troy.

"I line up in the slot," said Brendan. "Two steps back and halfway between Troy and the offensive line."

"Troy is my primary receiver, the first number I call in the huddle," said Drew.

"I run a Nine Route, break for the goalpost and make another break for the corner of the end zone," said Troy.

"No defensive backs have the footwork to cover the route," said Drew.

"Even if they did, Troy can out jump all of them," said Scott.

"My Nine Route is worth six points every game!" said Troy.

"That why the coach calls him—" said Drew.

"The Rob Gronkowski of Hingham!" they all said in unison.

"And if they double team me, then the defense has gotta deal with Brendan Foster!" said Troy.

"I run the Five Route, the Deep Out," Brendan said. "I run 10-15 yards downfield right between the linebackers and the defensive backs, and I cut ninety degrees to the sideline."

Drew imitated the coach's voice, "Where's the first down, Brendan? Look for the first down now, son."

Scott also impersonated their coach, "Make your sight adjustment, Brendan! Sight ad-just-ment!" The boys laughed.

"Try to take Troy away, and I'll be open every time," Brendan said. "My QB knows how to 'thread that needle'!"

"It only took me all summer to get it right," Drew said.

Scott impersonated their coach again, "Come on, Drew. 'Thread the needle' now. Over the linebackers and under the safeties. Over and under." This time Scott added the coach's hand gestures. The boys burst out laughing. Scott continued, "Hennings! What's the matter with you, son? Give him a chance to turn and run up field. Turn and run. Turn and run." Scott added more hand gestures. Brendan almost spit his drink all over his tray.

"I can't breathe," said Troy. "I can't breathe. It hurts so bad." The boys laughed harder than before.

Drew wiped his eyes. He tried to speak, and he had to stifle another laugh. He held up a hand before he spoke: "That said, when the recruiters call me, they always want to talk about the Deep Outs."

"They should be talking about how you run the ball. It's not just a pass, it's a *sprint* pass," said Brendan.

Drew smiled. "Drop back forty-five degrees to the right, clear the lineman, see the field, if no one's open, then tuck the ball and run."

"We're always open," said Troy.

"It's true," said Drew. "You fellas just make it so easy! Sometimes I get bored, so I keep the ball."

"You can switch places on the line with me any time," said Scott. "Have you really thrown for a touchdown and run for a touchdown in every game?"

"No," said Drew. His friends looked confused. "That's only fourteen points, and we score way more than that!" The boys cheered. Drew put his arm around Scott. "And we couldn't do it without the best O-line in the league!"

"And we're gonna keep your streak alive on Sunday night," said Scott. The bell rang, and the boys headed back to class.

Chapter 2
BETTER THAN EXPECTED

Will this day ever end? Drew thought. Friday afternoon lasted forever, but Friday night went by fast. The eight grade team went to the Hingham High School stadium to see their Harbormen play the North Quincy Red Raiders. It was cold, and both teams had had up-and-down seasons. The crowd was smaller than usual, but the boys had fun. *That's gonna be us next year*, Drew thought.

On Saturday, Drew woke up and went to practice. The team normally practiced at Lynch Field near the Shipyard. However, it was so cold that the team practiced inside. Since the Hingham Town Hall had once been Central Junior High School, there was a gymnasium inside. That is where the team completed its final walk through. Drew got home from practice, ate lunch, bundled up, and drove with his parents, Mike and Nancy, to watch his sister Libby play a sixth grade soccer game in Cohasset, the town bordering Hingham to the south. Drew stayed on the sideline for the first half. He tried to be a good big brother and pay attention, but he couldn't stop thinking about the Super Bowl. Drew started to shiver. *Am I nervous, or am I just cold?* he wondered. Drew's parents must have noticed because they let him watch the second half from the car.

Later that night the Hennings family hosted the team pasta party. The boys crowded into the basement, stuffed themselves full of pizza, pasta, and calzone, and watched old game film from elementary school. They laughed at themselves until Sprite dribbled out of the sides of their mouths. They changed from game film to football movies. They decided to watch Disney's *Little Giants.*

"A classic," said Scott.

"Drew, can you call the Annexation of Puerto Rico tomorrow?" asked Troy.

"First play of the second half?" asked Drew.

"That would be great. Thank you," said Troy.

"You know, Scott," said Drew. "Another play that we could steal from this movie is the One Cheek Sneak. You could blow a fart at the Duxbury defensive line, and I could run a QB sneak right up the middle. "

"You won't live long enough to take the snap," said Brendan.

"None of us will," said Troy.

The boys laughed and joked until the pasta party ended at ten o'clock. Drew often hosted the pasta parties, and his parents allowed it as long as he helped clean up afterward. When the last of his teammates had left, Drew walked to the basement door. Before he opened it, his Mom said, "Your Dad and I will clean up tonight. Get to bed."

"Really?" said Drew.

"Tomorrow's a big day. Get some rest," said Dad.

"Thanks," said Drew. He hugged his Mom and Dad.

"We're proud of you," said Mom.

"Thanks. Good night," said Drew.

Drew walked upstairs and got ready for bed. That night he lay awake for a long time. He wore a red Hingham Football t-shirt, and he rested his hands behind his head. He only pulled the covers up to his waist. Drew stared up at the ceiling, and he pictured himself making great plays in the Super Bowl. Hingham was going to be the home team, and Drew could easily recreate the field in his mind. He pictured himself throwing a touchdown pass to Troy. He saw himself jogging down the field and celebrating with his teammates in the end zone. Drew imagined himself making a long touchdown run. He saw himself hurdle the cornerback and stiff arm the safety. In his imagination all of this would happen in end zone near the scoreboard and the snack shack. In both scenarios he envisioned himself running to his right, directly in front of the Hingham sideline and their cheerleaders. Tomorrow Drew would be a Super Bowl champion, and coaches from the Independent School League and the Catholic Conference were going to ask him to commit to their schools. Maybe Callie would like him more when he was a champion. *I feel like a little kid on Christmas Eve*, he thought as he drifted happily off to sleep.

Drew slept late on Sunday morning, and his father woke him up just in time to eat breakfast and get dressed for church. The Hennings went to the Old Ship Church near Hingham Harbor, the oldest, continually-used wooden building on the North American continent. The Minister's sermon was about unity. Usually, Drew thought church was boring but peaceful. Today Drew felt like he was in prison. Drew could not sit still. He shifted in his seat over and over again. *I need one of those yoga balls that kids with ADHD get to sit on in school,* thought Drew. When the service finally ended, the Hennings shook hands with the Minister and thanked him. Mercifully, the Hennings skipped Coffee Hour at the Parish House across the street. The tradeoff, however, was that Drew had to go home and finish his homework. His Algebra and U.S. History homework would have been easy, but between every problem or question, Drew was answering texts from his teammates that read like, "Countdown to

Super Bowl trophy=2 hours." For English class Drew had to read a chapter from *A Separate Peace* and answer guided reading questions. He could not read more than a paragraph without zoning out or texting a teammate. Eventually, Drew stopped reading altogether. He just read the questions and skimmed the text for the answers. *Who cares if it's right? It's done,* he thought.

When he went downstairs for lunch, his family had prepared his favorite pre-game meal: chicken soup, bread and butter on the side, a banana, and a fruit punch sports drink. After he ate, Drew and his dad went outside to play catch. Drew warmed up with short throws and progressed to medium-range passes. In between throws Drew would try to keep his hands warm. *I better wear my hand warmer today,* he thought. Next, Drew jogged through his sprint out and practiced throwing the Deep Out route. Finally, he went upstairs to change for the game.

It was a short drive to Hingham High School. Daylight Savings Time had ended the week before. When Drew and his Dad arrived at 2:45pm, the parking lot closest to the stadium was nearly full, and the field lights were already on. Drew felt his stomach flip and a rush of adrenaline course through both of his forearms.

"I'll go back and get Mom and Libby," said Dad.

"Thanks, Dad," said Drew.

"I'm proud of you. Have fun out there today. Don't worry about anything else."

"Got it. Love you," said Drew. He grabbed his helmet and shoulder pads from the backseat, closed the door, and walked towards the practice field next to the stadium.

Most of the team was already there waiting for weigh-in. Drew quickly put on his gear and got in line. Duxbury had already weighed-in, and they were beginning warm-ups on the far side of the practice field. The only drama for Hingham was if Scott would make the cutoff. Scott was near the front of the line with his back to Drew. When Scott stepped on the scale, Drew heard him cheer, and his teammates at the head of the line also cheered. *So far, so good,* thought Drew.

As soon as the weigh-in was over, the Hingham backs and receivers took to the practice field to play catch and warm up. First, Drew jogged across the field and back throwing soft, ten-yard passes to Troy. He wanted to practice his footwork in case he was forced to throw on the run. Next, Drew did some ball-handling drills while the running backs did the same. Drew passed the ball from his right hand to his left hand, first around his head, then around his waist, then around his legs. *It's cold today. Ball security is key. Don't fumble,* he thought. Next, the entire backfield got together and jogged through some of their basic running plays. Finally, the backs lined up, and Drew practiced throwing them Fade Routes, or high, deep passes that usually target the back corner of the end zone. Drew always struggled with these passes. He could never get the nose of the ball to dip on its descent. *Tilt the ball in your hands. Flick your wrist. Imagine a giant funnel in the sky and throw into it,* he thought to himself. Drew had learned the techniques this past summer at Northeast Quarterback/ Receiver Camp at Lawrence Academy. The camp was also where he had gotten the attention of the coaches from Thayer, Milton and B.C. High.

Drew was able to throw three good Fade Routes in a row when the lineman finally joined the warm-up. Hingham warmed up quickly. The players did high knees, butt kicks, squats, lunges, and form jogging. Next, the team broke into small groups and completed footwork drills that were specific to their positions. Each position group also practiced light form blocking and form tackling drills. The warm-up ended with the entire offense running a few plays, and the entire defense running a few plays.

When the warm-up was over, the coach called the team together and reviewed the most important parts of the game plan. He said, "You've worked hard to be here. If you follow the plan, execute your assignments, and play together, then I think that this season is going to end just the way you want it to end. Captains, break them down."

The coaches walked toward the stadium and left Troy, Scott, Brendan, and Drew to talk to the team. The players stood up and surrounded their Captains.

"Duxbury hasn't lost in four years. That ends tonight!" said Troy.

"Fellas, we've got forty minutes left in the season, and the rest of the year to think about it. Leave it all out there on the field!" added Drew.

"What do we want?" shouted Scott.

"All I've got!" said the team.

"What do we want!" shouted Brendan.

"All I've got!" said the team.

"What do we want!" said Troy.

"All I've got!" shouted the team.

"Bring it in!" shouted Drew.

The team raised their right fists to the center of the circle.

"One, two, three!" said Drew.

"Harbormen!" they shouted together.

The boys turned and jogged towards the stadium. They stopped when they reached the entrance at the north end zone.

The cheerleaders had created a giant sign that read "Let's Go Hingham!" The players were a pulsing black and red mob behind the sign. Troy, Scott, and Drew pushed their way through the crowd to lead the team onto the field.

I hope no one steps on my feet, thought Drew. Then the announcer said, "And now, ladies and gentleman, please put your hands together for your own Hingham Harbormen!" Drew, Scott, Brendan and Troy burst through the sign with the team close behind them. Their jog to the sideline was short, and the Captains immediately lined up at midfield for the coin toss. The referees were standing at midfield, and one of them said, "Bring 'em in!"

The boys walked in unison to the center. The Duxbury Captains approached from the opposite side. They were dressed in white jerseys and green pants. Their helmets were silver with a big, green D on either side and green and white racing stripes down the center. The Captains from both teams shook hands and listened attentively to the referee's introductions and instructions. He tossed the coin, and Duxbury lost.

"We want the ball," said Drew. He stared right at the Duxbury Captain opposite him. Neither boy flinched. Next, the referee signaled the outcome of the coin toss to the crowd. The Captains shook hands one final time and went to their benches. Again the teams huddled and chanted. This cheer was not about team spirit; it was about intimidation. *Don't shout yourself hoarse. You've gotta to talk all night,* thought Drew.

Brendan caught the opening kickoff for Hingham and made a great return to the forty-three yard line. Drew handed the ball off twice to Brendan, and the Harbormen had a first down in Duxbury territory at the Green Dragon forty-two.

Drew came to the huddle and said, "Slot Right 95 Sprint Pass."

"Oh, yeah!" said Brendan.

The Harbormen broke the huddle. Drew was the last to get into position. He went through his pre-snap routine. Drew had gone through his pre-snap routine before every play all season, hundreds of repetitions. The whole exercise took fewer than fifteen seconds. *My guys are in the right positions. Looks like Duxbury is playing a 4-3 defense, four defensive lineman and three linebackers, same as always,* he thought to himself. Drew looked over the Duxbury defensive secondary starting from his right and moving to the left. *The corners are playing off and to the outside of Troy and Brendan. That means it's zone coverage. There's only one defender guarding Troy's area of the field. The Safety is going to move down and try to cover Brendan, and the outside linebacker will probably try to "stay home" and cover me,* thought Drew. Drew already had all of the information that he needed, but he looked to his left for a long time, *Make 'em think we're going that way,* Drew thought. He smiled because he knew exactly what was going to happen next.

Drew called the signals, took the snap, and sprinted to his right. He easily ran outside of the lineman, and he looked at his first read. Troy had already cut for the goal post, and the defender was a step behind him. Drew threw the ball high and deep towards the goal line pylon. As Drew released the ball, Troy cut to the outside corner. The defender spun around to stay with Troy, but the spin put more distance between them. Troy sped up, ran right underneath the ball, caught it, and cruised to the end zone for a touchdown. Drew threw his hands in the air, and the crowd roared.

Just like I imagined it last night! thought Drew as he jogged down the Hingham sideline to celebrate with his teammates in the end zone.

He heard the cheerleaders call "Go, Drew!" as he ran by. Drew looked right at Callie and smiled. He couldn't help himself.

"Go, Hingham!" said Callie.

Come on! Say 'Go Drew!' he thought. Drew met Troy in the end zone. They jumped as high as they could, turning slightly in the air so that their shoulders bumped. It was the only form of celebration that the referees still allowed. Troy handed the ball to the nearest official, and he and Drew ran upfield to hug Scott.

Scott's face was bright red. "Yeah, baby! That's how we do it!" he shouted.

Hingham lined up for the extra point. Scott was very athletic, and he did all of the team's kicking and punting. Troy was the long snapper, and Drew was the holder. Drew took his place and put his left index finger in the turf. Scott put his kicking foot right against Drew's finger. He liked the ball leaning slightly to the right, and Scott did not want to kick the laces.

"Laces out and lean right," said Drew.

"Yes, please," said Scott as he took three big steps back and two sideways and to the left. Drew watched Scott get set. When Scott was ready, he nodded at Drew, and Drew nodded back. Drew turned towards Troy, stuck out his right hand to give Troy a target and yelled, "Set!"

Troy fired back a perfect spiral directly at Drew's hand. Drew deftly caught the ball and placed it exactly where Scott wanted it. Scott kicked the ball and sent it straight between the uprights and into the net behind them. The execution was precise and perfect, and the kick looked like it would have been good from forty yards away. Troy, Scott, and Drew hugged.

Scott blasted the ensuing kickoff, but a good return gave Duxbury the ball at their own thirty-seven yard line. Drew jogged out to his position as the free safety. He lined up twelve yards away from the line of scrimmage in the middle of the field. Duxbury broke the huddle and lined up in a slot formation, just as Hingham had done on their touchdown play. Drew cheated over a few steps towards the Duxbury receivers. The quarterback took the snap. Drew kept one eye on the wide receiver and the other on the quarterback. The wide receiver sprinted forward as fast as he could. Drew also saw the quarterback's front shoulder rise like he was getting ready to throw. Drew stayed low and back peddled as fast as he could. In an instant the Duxbury quarterback lobbed a high, deep pass towards the wide receiver, a Fade Route. Drew took a big step back and to his left and sprinted towards the wide receiver. It was Brendan Foster's job to cover the wide receiver, but the receiver had him beat by one step. Drew sprinted to close the gap between him and the others, and he angled his body so that he would run just beyond the receiver. Drew was just three steps away when he saw the receiver stretch out both arms. The ball was coming! Drew looked over his right shoulder and leapt. Drew got his hands up in time to catch the ball. He brought it to his chest and tried to stomp one foot on the ground before he fell out of bounds. He looked up, and the official was standing over him waving his arms back and forth, "He's out of bounds! No catch! No catch!"

Drew didn't have time to react because Brendan Foster was in his face, "Great play, baby! Whoo! That pick's yours next time!"

Drew tossed the ball to the official, got up, and jogged back to the huddle. After that Duxbury chose to run the ball. They drove steadily down the field. Drew assisted on a couple of tackles. Eventually the Green Dragons drove inside Hingham's twenty-yard line, the Red Zone. When Hingham was on defense, the coach substituted Drew in and out of the game so that he could rest. When opposing teams made it into the Red Zone, Drew always came out of the game. A few plays after Drew went to the sideline, Duxbury broke though Hingham's defensive line for a touchdown. Their extra point tied the game at seven with only seconds left in the first quarter.

The teams traded punts until there were two minutes and thirty seconds left to go in the first half. Duxbury punted the ball, and Brendan fielded it on his own thirty-yard line. He made the first defender miss and ran the ball all the way to the Duxbury forty-eight. As the Harbormen jogged to their offensive huddle, the coach told Drew, "Line them up in Slot Right 95 Sprint Pass. During your pre-snap routine, if you see the middle linebacker cheat over towards the receivers, tap the center and sneak the ball up the middle." Drew jogged to the huddle and gave the team the play. When Hingham lined up, the Duxbury middle linebacker did exactly what Drew's coach said he would do. Drew finished his pre-snap routine. Before he got into position to take the snap, he tapped the center on his left hip. As soon as Drew's hands were in place to take the snap, the center hiked the ball. Drew tucked the ball and stepped between the center and the left guard. The defensive lineman were caught completely off guard, and Drew cleared them in one step. The linebackers frantically tried to tackle Drew, and they ran into each other. Drew ran towards the strong safety. With one cut to his right and a stiff arm, Drew was in the open field. It was a sprint to the goal line, and Drew had to beat the free safety and the left cornerback. Drew's facemask appeared to bounce up in down just in front of him, and all that he could hear was the whistle of the air through his helmet and the high-pitched cheers of the fans. As Drew crossed the goal line, he felt the fingertips of the free safety graze his heals. The cornerback never had a chance. Drew tossed the football to the official who had just arrived at the goal line. The official raised his hands to signal touchdown, and the football bounced off of his chest.

Scott was the first player to hug Drew, "They barely touched you! That's embarrassing!"

Drew didn't know what to say. A forty-eight-yard Quarterback Sneak for a touchdown: it was unheard of! Drew didn't have to say anything because just then he was mobbed by the rest of the team. After the celebration, Scott kicked the extra point. The Hingham defense held, and the Harbormen went to halftime with a 14-7 lead.

Chapter 3

THINGS CHANGE

Drew and his teammates jogged to the corner of the south end zone. As Drew jogged by the cheerleaders, he smiled at Callie, "Good luck," he said.

"Thanks," she said, and she smiled back at him.

Drew looked at the crowd. He saw the coaches who were recruiting him standing along the fence that separated the field from the stands. He saw the black and orange of the Thayer Academy Coach, and Drew saw the navy blue and orange of the Coach from Milton Academy. The B.C. High Coach was standing next to them, and he was wearing maroon and gold. Then Drew saw something that made him do a double take. There was a fourth coach who had come to watch the game, and he wore the blue and gold of the Hawks of Xaverian Brothers High School. Xaverian was an all-boys Catholic school west of Boston. Massachusetts is not known for high school football like Texas, Pennsylvania, Ohio, or Florida; however, there are exceptions. The Xaverian Hawks were one of them. They played in the state finals at Gillette Stadium every year, and every year they sent several players to Division One college football programs all over the country. Several Xaverian alumni had played professional football, and as a rule the sons of retired New England Patriots played at Xaverian. *Is the Xaverian coach here to watch me?* thought Drew. Xaverian was not the type of school that needed to recruit. They were so talented and so deep that they usually attacked their opponents in waves. There was barely a difference in the play of the starters and their back-ups.

When the Harbormen had assembled in the end zone, their Head Coach addressed the team, "Great first half, men. Remember, in football things can change pretty fast. This Duxbury team knows how to win, and we know that they won't let up until the final whistle. Stay focused; follow the game plan; play together, and I think that you're going to like how this one ends. I only want to make one change on defense. Coach-"

The Defensive Coordinator spoke next. He explained that Troy, an outside linebacker on defense, was going to switch positions and become a defensive end and play from a three point stance. He said, "Troy, I need you to follow their star running back. Whichever side he lines up on I want you to line up on that side too. Switch with the other defensive end when you have to. Also, when it's an obvious passing situation, I want you to start in a three point stance and at the snap drop into your usual position. We want to shut down their run game and dare them to throw in the second half. They need to score at least twice to win, and if we take away their best plays, then we might force them to make a mistake that can win us the game."

The Head Coach spoke again, "Rest. Relax. It's cold out here, so in three minutes let's do a quick warm-up."

As soon as the Coach ended the meeting, Drew heard his Dad calling him from behind the fence. Drew jogged over. Mr. Hennings was standing among the high school coaches.

"Gentlemen, this is my son, Drew," said Mr. Hennings.

Drew and his father had prepared for this moment, "It's a pleasure to meet you. Thank you very much or coming."

"You're playing a great game out there, young man," said the Thayer Academy Coach.

"Thank you," Drew replied.

"That touchdown pass was right 'on the money.' I could sure use a quarterback who can throw like that," said the Milton Academy Coach.

Before Drew could respond the B.C. High Coach said, "You were so close to making that interception. I love a defensive player who has a 'nose for the ball.'"

"Thank you," said Drew.

"And I think that I can speak for all of the coaches here when I tell you that we cannot remember the last time that we saw a fifty-yard touchdown run on a Quarterback Sneak," said the Coach from Xaverian.

"Thanks," said Drew. "We were hoping to catch them off guard with that one."

"You certainly did, Drew," said the Xaverian Coach.

"Thanks," Drew replied. Just then the Hingham coaches blew their whistles to signal that it was time to warm-up.

"It was very nice to meet you all," said Drew. He turned to jog onto the field, and he stopped suddenly. Just as his father had told him, Drew turned and said, "Thanks again for coming." Drew turned and jogged onto the field. He heard a jumble of salutations, but he was not sure who had said what.

Shortly afterward the second half began. Duxbury was on offense, but they went nowhere. In his new role, Troy was more of a menace to the Duxbury run game than ever. Next, the Hingham offense took over. The Harbormen moved the ball, but they could not finish drives and add to their score. When the third quarter ended, the score remained 14-7 with Hingham in the lead.

As the fourth quarter got under way, things changed. Hingham lined up in a punt formation. Troy fired the long snap back to Scott who began his kick. From the sideline Drew heard the punter's foot connect with the ball, "Boom!" The sound was immediately followed by another, "Boom!" Seemingly out of nowhere, a Duxbury defender had sprinted from the edge of Hingham's formation, dove, and blocked the kick. All of the Hingham players were already running downfield to cover the punt that never happened. The ball took a lucky bounce right into the arms of another Duxbury player who jogged into the end zone for an easy touchdown. The Green Dragon fans erupted in cheers, and the Hingham fans groaned.

The score was 14-13, and a Duxbury extra point would tie the game with five minutes and twenty seconds to go. However, the Green Dragons were not looking to tie the game. They sent their offense out to try for a two-point conversion.

"Timeout!" shouted the Hingham Head Coach as he sprinted down the sideline to find a referee. The Hingham coaches set up their goal line defense, the defense that Drew did not play, and the teams lined up for the two-point conversion. When the Duxbury quarterback took the snap, he sprinted to his right as if to hand off to their star running back. The entire Hingham defense followed. At the instant that the quarterback was supposed to hand the ball to his teammate, he stopped pivoted to his left and threw a bullet to the back of the end zone. Duxbury's left tight end was standing all alone, and he caught the pass without any challenge from the Harbormen. He had faked like he was run blocking and had snuck behind the Hingham defenders.

It was the right play called at exactly the right time, and it had been executed perfectly. The Duxbury Green Dragons took their first lead of the game, 15-14.

Drew tried to lift up his teammates as they came to the sideline, "It's cool. We've got this! Plenty of time!" For the first time all night Drew could see the fear and doubt in their eyes. Drew's stomach turned. Duxbury kicked off, and Brendan could not get very far. The Harbormen took over on their own twenty-five-yard line with just more than five minutes left in the game. Just after Drew and his teammates huddled in the middle of the field, the officials called timeout to fix a problem with the game clock. Drew looked at his teammates, and they still looked nervous. He reached into the hand warmer that he wore around his waist and took out some chap stick. Drew took his helmet off and put on the chap stick. He made sure to smack his lips a few times before he said, "Do I look pretty? I want to look pretty."

His teammates looked back at him in stunned silence.

"After we score this touchdown, I'm gonna plant a big 'ol wet one on yuh, Scotty Boy!"

The boys burst out laughing. Just then the referee blew the whistle to resume the game, and the Hingham players jogged to the line. Some of them were still chuckling.

The Hingham offense quickly found its rhythm. They kept the ball on the ground, and the Duxbury defense started to show signs of wearing down. Hingham alternated the runners: the fullback, Brendan Foster, and Drew. They ran left; they ran right. They ran inside; they ran outside. Troy lived up to his reputation as Hingham's little Rob Gronkowski, and Scott lead the surge off of the line of scrimmage. Soon it was first and goal at the ten for the Harbormen with one minute and forty seconds remaining in the game. Drew took the ball around the left end for a two-yard gain. It was second and goal from the eight with one minute and twelve seconds remaining. Hingham called its second timeout of the half. The coach called two plays. There was not enough time to huddle between them. After the timeout, Drew handed the ball off to Brendan, and Brendan was stuffed at the line of scrimmage for no gain. As the players got up off of the ground, the clock continued to run: fifty-nine seconds, fifty-eight, fifty-seven. The crowd got louder and louder. Drew nearly shouted himself hoarse trying to get his teammates lined up for the second play. Hingham finally lined up in a Slot Left formation and snapped the ball with forty-six seconds left to play in the game. Drew spun to his left and tossed the ball back to his tailback. On the outside Troy and Brendan blocked the defensive backs in front of them. Scott and the left guard pulled to their left. Drew sprinted down the left side of the line to join the convoy of blockers who were going to escort their teammate to the end zone. However, the toss sweep left did not work out that way. Duxbury's middle linebacker "shot the gap" left by Scott and the left guard, raced in behind the wall of blockers and smothered Hingham's tailback at the eleven yard line.

The Hingham crowd groaned. Drew looked to the sideline at his Head Coach. The Head Coach put both hands out as if to say, "Stay calm."

"Get them in the huddle, Drew!" he shouted.

What! thought Drew. *There isn't time! Have you lost your mind?* The referee quickly spotted the ball and signaled that the officials were ready for the next play. There were twenty-nine seconds left on the clock. The Hingham Head Coach jogged down the sideline and stood next to the wing official. Together they watched the seconds tick down. Drew remembered that his team had one timeout left, and he relaxed. He looked at his teammates, and he said, "He's making sure that this is the last play of the game. We're not giving Duxbury a chance to get the ball back."

When the clock reached nine seconds, Hingham's Head Coach called his final timeout. The sideline official blew his whistle and touched his fingertips to his shoulders, "That's Hingham's final timeout. It's a thirty-second timeout."

Drew jogged over to his Coach. He was alone, and the eyes of the entire stadium were fixed on both of them. It was hard for Drew to look up at his Coach because Drew got blinded by the stadium lights. Drew bent his head and leaned his left ear towards the Coach. Drew barely heard the name of the play over the cow bells, spirit horns, and stomping feet. He repeated the play back to the Coach to make sure that he got it right. Drew could see his breath rise through his face mask. He turned and jogged back to his huddle. The 30 second timeout was over.

"Let's go, Drew!" The cheerleaders were on the sideline just behind Drew, and he instantly recognized Callie's voice. *Don't turn around. Focus,* he thought. Drew smiled in spite of himself. As he jogged near the huddle, all of his teammates' eyes were on him. Drew could feel their intensity.

"All you got! Right now! Let's go!" said Scott.

"The hay is in the barn, boys!" said Troy.

Drew smiled and quickly called the play, "Slot Right 95 Sprint Pass." The team broke the huddle. Although they were all exhausted, the offense nearly sprinted to the line of scrimmage. Drew waited for his teammates to get set, and he began his pre-snap routine. Drew surveyed the defense. Just like in the first quarter, Drew looked to his right and saw the Duxbury cornerback playing back and to the outside of Troy. The outside linebacker was lined up the same way against Brendan Foster. As Drew looked to his left, he thought, *They're still playing zone again. We've got this. I'm either going to throw it to Troy for a touchdown, or I'm going to run it in. There's no way that their linebacker can cover me.* What Drew did not see was the cornerback and the outside linebacker switch their coverage. Duxbury was using a "disguise," a quick change in their defensive alignment that tried to confuse the offense and force them to make a mistake. While Drew wasn't looking, the Duxbury defenders took one big step towards the middle of the field and a few little steps forward. Now they were covering Troy and Brendan "man-to-man." In this new defense, the safety was covering Drew, but Drew didn't know that. The change happened right in front of Hingham's bench. The Hingham coaches saw it, and they shouted frantically to try to get Drew's attention. Their cries were lost in the cheering of the crowd.

Drew stood under center, called his signals, and the center snapped the ball. Drew sprinted diagonally to his right, and looked at his first key, the cornerback covering Troy. Troy made his second cut and sprinted for the back of the end zone. The cornerback followed closely. Drew "checked down" to his second option, Brendan Foster, who was also covered. Drew looked for the outside linebacker who he thought was covering him. The outside linebacker was not there. Drew tucked the ball under his arm and sprinted towards the goal line pylon in the front of the end zone. He never looked to see what the Duxbury safety was doing. Drew did not think that he had to. Both Troy and Brendan saw Drew start to run. They turned and blocked. Drew ran as hard as he could for the pylon. He was going to dive for the score, just to be sure. He never saw the safety sprinting towards him, closing fast. Drew gripped the ball with both arms and leapt for the end zone. Then everything went black.

Chapter 4

WAITING

Drew heard an unfamiliar voice, and it sounded like it was underwater. The voice was saying the same thing over and over again, but it took a while for Drew to make sense of what he heard, "Drew, can you hear me? Can you hear me, Drew?"

Drew opened his eyes, and he saw a really bright light. His vision was blurry, and as it came back into focus, Drew could tell that the light came from a flashlight that was moving back and forth in front of his face.

"His eyes are opened," said the voice. It continued, "Pupils are dilated. He's got a concussion at least. Drew, if you can hear me, then I want you to blink your eyes, ok?"

Drew blinked his eyes.

"My name is Rick. I'm an E.M.T. You took a big hit out there. I just want to check and see if you're ok. Blink if you understand me."

Drew blinked again.

Rick spoke again, "I want to ask you a few questions, and I want you to tell me the answers, ok?"

"Ok," said Drew.

"Good," said Rick. "Can you tell me your name?"

"Drew Hennings"

"How old are you?" asked Rick.

"I'm fourteen," said Drew.

"What town do you live in?"

"Hingham."

"What day is it today?"

Drew had to think for a minute. "It's Sunday." *The Game!* he thought.

"Good," said Rick. "Now I want you to…"

"The game!" said Drew. "Is it over? Did we win?"

"Easy, Drew. Your Dad is here with us. He can tell you everything that you want to know, but you have to let me do my job first, ok?" asked Rick. He did not wait for a response. "Can you count down from ten for me, please?"

Drew did as he was asked. His answer was slow, and as he continued to count down, his head began to throb. Rick noticed Drew begin to wince in pain.

"Drew, I'm going to hold your left hand in my hand. You can see me holding your hand. Now, squeeze my hand."

Drew did as he was told.

"That's a great grip," said Rick.

Off to Drew's right, another voice said, "That's great, Drew!"

Drew instantly recognized his Dad's voice. He tried to look in his Dad's direction, but he couldn't move his head. *What's going on?* he thought. Drew's eyes grew wide.

Rick said, "Just focus on me for a little while longer, ok?"

Rick checked Drew's right hand, and he said, "An even better grip. That must be your throwing arm. You're doing great, Drew. Now, I want you to try to wiggle your feet. Start with your right foot, and then try and wiggle your left foot, ok?"

Drew wiggled his feet.

"You got hit on the head pretty hard, Drew," said Rick. "You were unconscious for a little while, maybe about ten minutes. We strapped you to a backboard, and you're on a gurney. The great news is that you can move your arms and legs. You still have all of your football gear on, but we did have to unfasten your facemask. If there is something wrong with your head or with your spine, then we do not want to jostle you around and make it worse. The ambulance is taking you to Weymouth to get an MRI. The doctors will take pictures of your skull and of your spine to make sure that nothing is wrong. We should be there in about five minutes. Do you have any questions for me?"

"No," said Drew.

"Alright, Dad. I'm done for now. I'll let you guys talk football," said Rick.

Suddenly Dad's face came into view against the white ceiling of the ambulance. "Hey, Drew," he said.

"Hey. Did I score? Did we win?"

Drew's Dad paused. Finally, he said, "When you ran for the pylon, the safety ran for the pylon. When you dove, he dove. Your helmets collided." Dad paused. "It didn't look to me like a dirty play. It was an accident. The guy who hit you got hurt too. He didn't get knocked out, but he definitely got a concussion."

"Did I get in?" asked Drew.

"I'm sorry, Drew. No. The ball popped loose as soon as you got hit. Duxbury won."

Drew's eyes filled with tears. He couldn't wipe them away, and he couldn't even turn to hide his face. Dad held Drew's hand and said nothing.

After a few minutes, Rick said, "We're one minute out." He started to prepare Drew and Dad for what was going to happen next. "We called ahead, and they're expecting us. When we arrive, there are going to be two nurses to help us. I'm going to need you to be as quiet as you can because I need to tell them everything that I know about how you're doing. The lights inside can get pretty bright, so I might close your eyes, Drew. Dad, you're going to have to wait in the waiting room. You're going to need to fill out a little paperwork, but you should have plenty of time. These kind of MRIs take about an hour."

"Drew, I know you're upset about the game, and you have every right to be. But football doesn't matter right now. All that matters is that you're ok. Mom and Libby are on their way. I'll fill them in. You just stay calm and do exactly what the doctors and nurses tell you to do, ok?"

"Ok," said Drew.

The ambulance stopped. When the back doors opened, Drew felt a rush of cold, November air, and it gave him goosebumps. He heard Rick and his father get out, and then he heard new, unfamiliar voices. In moments Drew was inside and being rolled down a long hallway. Rick told the nurses and a doctor the whole story of Drew's injury and his condition. The doctor and the nurses asked a few, brisk questions. The group reached a double door, and Rick said goodbye, "It was nice to meet you, Drew. Good luck!"

"Thank you, Rick!" said Drew.

"No problem, pal," he replied. Rick turned and left.

"Hey, Drew. I'm Dr. Gwenn Parker. I'm a Radiologist. We're going to take some pictures of your head and back and make sure that you're ok." Dr. Parker wore navy blue scrubs that were dotted with the miniature logo of the New England Patriots. Her long, dark hair was pulled back, and she wore stylish glasses. "Drew, the nurses and I are just going to give you another quick check up to make sure that nothing's changed since Rick evaluated you. The doctor and the nurses went to work, and Dr.

Parker made small talk with Drew. "So you're from Hingham? Do you go to the high school?"

"Eighth grade," said Drew.

"They just built that new middle school over there. I drive by there all the time on my way to work. Is it really nice?"

"Yes," said Drew.

"Good. You kids deserve it. I live in Cohasset, and my kids are still in elementary school, but I bet that soon enough we'll be over there for soccer games and basketball games. I look forward to seeing the new school. I wish Cohasset would build a new middle school like that."

Drew smiled.

"So you play football. Are you the quarterback?" asked Dr. Parker.

"Yes," said Drew.

"Who were you playing today?"

"Duxbury," said Drew.

"Did you score any touchdowns?" asked Dr. Parker.

"I threw for one, and I ran for one," said Drew.

"Well done. Congratulations," said Dr. Parker.

"Thanks," said Drew.

"And he's got a great smile too. Should we get some extra chairs in the waiting room for all of the girls who are going to want to know that he's ok?" asked Dr. Parker.

Drew smiled. *Is it weird to have a crush on your doctor*, Drew thought?

"So let me tell you what is about to happen. We're going to put you into the MRI machine. We knew that you were coming, and we reserved the new one for you. It's roomier than the older ones. The machine buzzes a lot, but don't worry about that. I

33

know that you've got a pretty bad headache, but we're going to ask you to listen to some soft music. The reason we do that is because we want to keep you awake until we know exactly what is going on. One of us will be in the Control Room right next door, and we'll check in on you. If you need anything, or if you need a break, then just say so. We can hear you from the Control Room. One last thing: I know that you've been strapped to that board for a long time, and I know that the MRI machine is not the most comfortable place to be in the world, but please try to stay as still as you can, ok? It will help us get the pictures that we need to make sure that you're ok. Do you have any questions?"

Drew didn't have any questions. Dr. Parker and the nurses moved Drew and his backboard from the gurney to the big, metal slab on the MRI machine. Dr. Parker and her colleague left the room, and one of the nurses remained to help Drew. She adjusted a set of headphones to fit over his football helmet, she covered him with a thin blanket, and she pressed a button. The big, metal slab that Drew was lying on began to move slowly into the tunnel of the giant machine. When Drew was finally inside, there were soft lights on either side of him, and his nose was about eighteen inches from the ceiling of the tunnel. He heard the nurse's voice in the headphones, "What radio station do you want to listen to?"

"Anything. It doesn't matter to me," Drew replied.

"How about Kiss 108?" asked the nurse.

"Sure. Thanks," said Drew.

"Remember. Try as hard as you can to stay awake ok?"

"Yes," said Drew.

The music came on. Drew lay there and listened to the music and to the hum of the machine. He felt uncomfortable and gross. *I would do anything for a shower right now,* he thought. *What time is it? Will I have to go to school tomorrow?*

After a few minutes the DJ introduced Sia's hit song, "The Greatest," and she said, "I just had a request for this song from Duxbury Youth Football. Congrats on your Super Bowl championship and on four consecutive undefeated seasons!"

Drew cried again. He tried to be as quiet as possible, but the Nurse interrupted the song and said, "Everything alright in there?"

Drew stopped long enough to say, "Fine." After that she left him alone.

When the MRI finally ended, Drew felt like he had been let out of prison. As the nurses transferred him back onto the gurney, he asked them, "Can I walk now?"

"You've been very patient. The doctors are looking at your film now. We're going to wheel you into the hallway, and they'll be with you in a few minutes," said the Nurse.

"Can I sleep?" Drew asked.

"Try to stay awake, ok? It'll just be a little while longer," said the nurse.

Drew stared at the ceiling tiles and tried to keep himself awake. *Shower, ice cream, NFL Sunday Night Football, bed,* he thought. It felt to Drew like a long time before Dr. Parker came out of the control room.

"Drew, I've got great news: no broken bones, no bleeding in your brain. You're going to go home tonight," she said.

"Great. Can I get up now?" asked Drew.

"Absolutely," said Dr. Parker. "I'll tell you what we are going to do. The nurses will help you get back on your feet. You might feel a bit dizzy, so take your time. They'll escort you to your family in the waiting room. I'm going to go ahead and catch them up on everything that's been going on."

"Thanks, Doc," said Drew.

"You're welcome. I'll see you in just a few minutes."

"Ok," said Drew. Dr. Parker left, and the nurses helped release Drew from the backboard. The hardest part was working with the two of them to get his helmet off. When Drew finally sat up, he felt dizzy.

"Just sit here for a minute until you feel better. We'll get you some juice," said the nurse.

Drew sipped cranberry juice with ice chips in it, and after a few minutes he felt good enough to try walking. He walked up and down the hall with the nurses on either side of him. He felt very sore, but he had no other trouble.

"Are you ready to see your family now?" asked the other nurse.

"Yeah. Let's go," said Drew. He walked slowly out into the waiting room with the nurses just behind him. He saw Dr. Parker talking to his Mom, Dad, and Libby. As soon as Drew's Mom saw him, she excused herself from the conversation and rushed towards her son. She stopped short just in front of him. Tears were already streaming down her cheeks. "Oh, thank God," she said. Mom put her hands on Drew's cheeks and inspected him like he was a child going off to Sunday School. She sobbed, "I was so scared. I thought you weren't going to walk again." She put her head on her son's shoulder and cried.

"I'm ok, Mom," Drew said. He choked up.

Mom could sense her son's emotion, and she quickly got a hold of herself. By this time Libby and Dad were hugging Drew too.

"You need a shower. You smell terrible," said Mom between sniffles.

Dr. Parker came over and said, "I'm sorry to interrupt. If you have any questions, here's how to reach me." She handed her card to Drew's Dad. "Drew, you've got a bad concussion. The dizziness and the headaches are going to come and go for a little while. It might take a long time until you feel back to normal again, so take it easy, ok? Have a safe trip home, you guys,"

"Thank you, Doctor," said Dad. The Hennings said their goodbyes and left. The drive home was quick and quiet. They were tired, but they were happy to be together. Despite his protests, Mom and Libby escorted Drew into the house. Dad pulled the car into the garage, turned off the ignition, pressed the button to close the garage door, and cried.

Chapter 5
RECOVERY

In the week after the injury Drew had many visitors because all of his teammates wanted to make sure that he was ok. He even received a get well card from Callie. Drew did not go back to school until after Thanksgiving break. Drew's doctor told him to sleep as much as he could, and Drew was not allowed to do any school work except a little reading. Drew would not have minded it so much except that he was not allowed to watch television, use a computer, or use his phone. When Drew was awake, he was allowed to lie down in the dark. He did not have to try hard to follow his doctor's orders because the darkest day of the year was only three weeks away. Drew slowly noticed that his symptoms were improving, however, he was sleeping a lot more than he normally did; he wasn't active, and he didn't see his friends very often.

Drew tried to spend the time as best he could. He played board games with his family, and when his mom went out, he snuck onto his tablet and watched the film of the Super Bowl game. Every time he watched the game film Drew hoped that he could somehow rewrite the ending. At least watching it made him feel something. While he had trouble accepting the outcome, Drew had no trouble forgiving himself for fumbling the ball. Even on film, the collision that knocked him out looked scary. *Mom made a scene that night in the waiting room, but I can't really blame her,* he thought.

After Thanksgiving, Drew returned to school for half days. On the first day, he was overwhelmed by the attention and well wishes of his friends, but middle school gossip changes fast, and Drew was soon old news. In addition, Drew found his return to classes surprisingly difficult. He was not an enthusiastic student to begin with, and he realized quickly that he was hopelessly behind his classmates. Even though all of his teachers worked with the Hennings and Drew's guidance counselor to prioritize his work, he felt anxious in every class. His headaches came back, and no matter how many hours he slept at night Drew went through the motions of his morning classes like he was half asleep. By lunchtime, when his mom picked him up, he was totally exhausted. When he got home, Drew would nap for hours. When he wasn't asleep, Drew got so bored that he actually read all of his assigned text, John Steinbeck's, *The Pearl.* It was the first school book that he had read all the way through since the fall of seventh grade. Drew's parents helped him with his make-up work for History and Physical Science. Mrs. Hennings asked a neighbor, Claire Murray, to tutor Drew in math. Claire was also in the eighth grade, and she and Drew had known each other since they were little. They had been together at every Fourth of July cookout that Drew could remember.

In the second week of December, Drew went to school for lunch and afternoon classes. When he walked into the cafeteria for the first time in a month, he had never been happier in his life to see the place. As he walked to his table, his head started to hurt. *I forgot how loud it was in here,* he thought. No one noticed him. When he got there, Scott said, "Fellas, move over. Drew's back!"

Drew took a seat, but it wasn't his old seat.

"Are you feeling better?" Brendan asked.

"I'm alright. All I do is sleep all day. What have you been up to?" said Drew.

"My Dad built a rink in my back yard. I got to use it last night!" said Brendan.

"What about you guys?" asked Drew.

"Madden every day and lax on the weekends," said Troy.

"Same," said Scott.

"I miss video games," said Drew.

"What?" said Scott. "You can't play Madden?"

"No screens except for school," said Drew.

"That's rough," said Troy.

"Yeah," said Drew. "But when my parents aren't around, I've watched the Super Bowl film a couple of times."

"Really?" said Scott. "I don't ever want to watch that film."

"Neither do I," said Troy.

"No way," said Brendan. "I hate Duxbury."

"When I was at the hospital, the doctor let me listen to the radio. A Duxbury Fan called in and requested 'The Greatest.' They didn't lose a single game for four years," said Drew.

"Whatever. My Madden team is nasty," said Troy.

"Not as good as mine," said Scott.

The conversation moved on to video games and holiday presents. *What's with these guys?* Drew thought. *They love to talk about football.*

There was one bright spot in Drew's return to lunch. As he was walking out of the cafeteria, Callie said "hi" to him. However, Drew noticed that she was wearing a red high school hockey sweater. *If only I had scored that last touchdown!* he thought.

After school Claire came over to tutor Drew in Algebra I. They worked in the kitchen, and Claire helped Drew draw a graph for the function $y=2x+1$.

"I don't get it," said Drew. "It doesn't look like a line. I start at one on the y-axis, and I plug in one to the equation. Two times one is two. Plus one is three. So I draw a line over to three on the x-axis. When I do the same thing for the number two, then I draw another line over to five on the x-axis. This is a bunch of lines. The graph looks like a kindergartener trying to draw a sun."

"You've got it backwards, Drew," said Claire. "You start on the x-axis. Let me show you: I start at zero, and I plug it into the equation. Two times zero is zero. Plus one is one. I travel up the y-axis and draw a dot at one. Now, move over on the graph to x equals one. You try."

Drew completed the operations and got three.

"Move over one on the x-axis and go up to three on the y-axis," said Claire.

Drew did as he was told.

"Now draw a dot," said Claire

Drew made a dot.

"Connect the dots," said Claire.

Drew connected the dots.

"Now you have a line," said Claire.

"How many dots do I have to make before I'm done?"

"We usually draw five," said Claire.

Drew dropped his pencil, looked up at the ceiling, and took a deep breath. "This is giving me a headache. I've gotta stop," he said.

"Ok," said Claire. After math assignments, Claire would catch Drew up on gossip from school. Without his phone, she was his social lifeline. "I saw you at lunch today," she said. "It's been a while."

"Yeah," said Drew.

"Was it nice to see your friends again?" Claire asked.

Sometimes she sounds like my mom, Drew thought. "It was good. They didn't have too much to say. It was weird," said Drew.

"Oh," said Claire. "That's too bad." It was quiet for a moment and Claire said, "Callie told me that she saw you."

"Did she? Cool," said Drew. Drew put his head in his hands and pretended to have a headache. "Do you mind if I go upstairs?"

"Sure," said Claire.

"Thanks again for your help," said Drew.

"You're welcome," said Claire. She closed her book and her notebook, took her coat from the back of the chair, and put it on.

Drew didn't walk her to the door. His Mom would be mad at him, but he didn't care. Drew went up to his room and walked to the window. It was dark outside. Drew saw Claire walk out of the lamp light. He felt like a prisoner. He lay down on his bed and tried to sleep. He did not go down to dinner, and when Mom left a plate on his desk, he pretended to be asleep.

Christmas vacation finally arrived, and Drew got swept up in a blur of neighborhood and family parties. He was slowly feeling better. He even liked candlelight Christmas Eve service at Old Ship Church. The one down side of vacation was that after Christmas Drew's family decided to skip their annual ski trip to Sugarloaf Mountain in Carrabassett Valley, Maine. "If you hit your head again, then it will only make your recovery slower than it already is," said Dad and Mom.

"Come on, Dad. I was going to learn to snowboard on this trip," said Drew.

"Exactly," said Dad.

I have to give him that one, Drew thought. Drew continued to protest, but his parents would not budge. Drew was going to miss roasting S'mores by the giant fire pit on The Beach, and he would miss getting all of his friends together to go out for a Bag Burger. Instead Drew watched Libby and her sixth grade basketball team play in a local tournament. She played at a huge indoor sports complex in Hanover. It had a café and a video arcade. Drew remembered attending birthday parties there when he was in elementary school. He sat on the aluminum bleachers with his parents for as long as he could stand it. Sometimes he snuck off to an empty court and shot hoops. Sometimes his parents let him play video games in the arcade. It was lonely. All of Drew's friends were away.

Just before the New Year, Drew had a check-up with the doctor. He sat on the examination table. The room had choo-choo train wall paper. When he was little, he used to love the trains, but now it added to his discomfort. The doctor was a short woman with dark hair who had cared for Drew since he was an infant. Dr. Lewis checked his pupils, and she asked him to track her finger tip with his eyes. The doctor also asked him to count down from ten.

"Do you still get headaches very often?" she asked.

"No," said Drew.

"During your last visit you told me that you took a lot of naps after school. Do you still feel tired?" asked Dr. Lewis.

"Not really. Just bored," said Drew.

"He's been on school vacation," said Mom, who was sitting in a chair by the door.

The doctor addressed them both, "I know that it's been boring Drew, but it may have been the best thing for you. I think that you're ready to go back to school full time."

"Can I get my phone back?" Drew asked.

"I don't see why not," said Dr. Lewis.

"Yes!" said Drew. Mom and Dr. Lewis smiled.

"Nancy, he's making good progress, but he isn't completely healed yet. Please make sure that Drew limits his screen time. Our goal is to get Drew back to school for a full week without any significant discomfort. If he can do that, then we can add in homework," said Dr. Lewis.

They all shook hands.

"I'll see you again in two weeks?" Dr. Lewis asked.

"We'll schedule the appointment with the front desk," said Mom.

Drew smiled, "Thank you, Dr. Lewis."

"I've never seen you so happy to go to school," said Mom.

"Neither have I," said Drew. *I'm almost normal again,* he thought as he walked through the dark and the cold towards the car. It had been two months since he had been knocked unconscious.

One Saturday morning in early February, a brochure arrived for the Northeast Quarterback Receiver Camp. The whole family was in the kitchen.

"Dad, the brochure for quarterback camp is here. Can I sign up again?"

Drew's parents were sitting at the kitchen table. They looked at each other and said nothing. Libby sensed that an argument was coming, and she took a front row seat at the kitchen island.

"You said yourself that it was really helpful last year. Can I go?" asked Drew.

"Drew, why don't you have a seat?" said Dad.

"What's going on?" asked Drew.

"Just sit. We'll talk it over," said Dad.

"Talk what over? Did I do something wrong?" asked Drew.

Dad looked at Mom. The look that she gave him made it clear that it was Dad who was going to break the news to Drew. Dad looked at Drew, took a deep breath, and said, "Drew, your mother and I think it's best if you don't play football anymore. We—"

"This is a joke right? asked Drew.

His parents didn't answer.

"This is funny. Good one," said Drew.

His parents still didn't answer.

"Dad, this is the part where you say: surprise! You're not going to Quarterback Camp because we already signed you up for Brown University football camp instead," said Drew.

"We're not joking with you," said Dad.

"What! No!" said Drew.

"Drew, I know that you're upset. If you—" said Dad.

"Upset! You're upset. I got a concussion. That was almost three months ago. I'm fine!" said Drew.

"What we're trying to say is—"

"I'm not interested in what you're saying. It's what you're doing that's a problem. You're trying to ruin my life! I want to play high school football next year with all of my friends. I want to play football in college, Dad, just like you did. Don't you care what I want? Don't you want me to be happy?" Drew asked.

"May I please speak?" asked Dad. Drew knew from his father's body language that the conversation had reached a critical point. In the background, Libby was hanging on every word. Drew glared at his father and said nothing.

"Drew, we love football, and we love watching you play. We know that you're good at it, and we know that it makes you happy. We also know that your injury was an exception and not the rule, but we have to face the fact that it happened. Drew, it took more than two months for you to recover," said Dad.

"You couldn't go to school. You couldn't do homework. You fell way behind," said Mom.

"You couldn't exercise. You didn't see much of your friends. You walked around here like a zombie," said Dad.

"Drew, the life you've lead the last couple of months is no life at all. Your father and I want better for you," said Mom.

"It's our job to make sure that you're safe," said Dad.

"But dad, I'm fine," said Drew.

"It's not a broken bone or a sprained ankle we're talking about here," said Dad. "This is your brain, the most important part of your body. We've got to take steps to make sure that you're safe. Your mother and I have been talking, and we decided that we are going to limit your exposure to contact sports. You may continue to play lacrosse. There is a lot less hitting than there is in football, but football is over. "

Yelling had not worked, and Drew tried pleading, "Dad, please don't do this. Football's my favorite sport. My dream is to play college ball like you did. Please?"

"No. I'm sorry," said Dad.

"Mom? Please?"

"No," said Mom.

Drew stood up and turned to leave.

"Sit!" said Dad.

Drew arched his back and stopped.

Dad calmed himself and said, "Drew, I know that you need some time alone to take this all in. I'm only asking for a little while longer."

Nobody moved.

"Drew, if you leave before everything has been said, then we're just going to have to drag this out. You don't want that. We don't want that," said Dad.

Drew turned around and took his seat. He did not look up.

"Thank you," said Dad. "Drew, I know that you're angry at us, and that you may be angry at us for a long time. I just wanted you to know—I just have to tell you what it was like for me the night that you got hurt." Dad took a deep breath and continued, "You know that you were unconscious for ten minutes. You don't remember any of that, but I do. I remember watching the E.M.T's strapping you to a backboard; I remember sitting beside you in an ambulance and thinking that you were going to live the rest of your life sitting in a wheelchair and breathing through a tube and eating through a straw. I thought that I was going to be sick. Go ahead and hate me if you want to." Dad and Drew were looking right at each other. Drew could see tears in his father's eyes. Dad's voice was shaky, but he said, "I am your father. My job is to keep you safe. I am never letting you go through that again. I am never letting this family go through something like that again."

There was a long silence.

"May I go now?" asked Drew.

"Yes," said Dad.

Drew rose and began to walk out of the kitchen. He stopped halfway and turned back to his parents, "What am I going to tell the coaches who recruited me?" he asked.

"I already took care of that," said Mom.

Drew nodded and walked out of the kitchen.

Chapter 6

"...IN THESE THOUGHTS MYSELF ALMOST DESPISING"
SONNET 29 BY WILLIAM SHAKESPEARE

February and March were tense times in the Hennings household. Drew tried several times to convince his parents to reconsider, but they would not change their minds. In the spring, Drew returned to lacrosse, and he channeled all of his anger and frustration into it. He played well, and the team played well. They played an away game against Duxbury, and they won it.

After the celebration Drew walked off the field with Brendan, Scott, and Troy. Scott put his arm around Drew and said, "I hope they liked a little payback."

Drew smiled at Scott. It was the first time since December that any of his friends had mentioned their Super Bowl loss.

"We'll beat them in the fall too," said Troy.

"That's right!" said Brendan.

Drew was silent, and he felt his stomach do a flip. He did not talk with anyone about quitting football. Drew tried not to think about it.

Summer arrived. Quarterback camp was usually right after the Fourth of July. To take Drew's mind off of football, Drew's parents rescheduled their family trip to New Hampshire. Instead of quarterback camp, Drew was vacationing at the Mount Washington Resort Hotel. He hiked, played golf, swam, and flirted with pretty girls at the pool. He even tried horseback riding. *That was scary. I'm not going to lie, and I can't believe how much horses poop!* he thought. It was an awesome vacation, and Drew did not miss quarterback camp. However, as he rode home through the White Mountain National Forest, Drew put his headphones in and rolled the windows down. The air felt fresh and cool, and Drew could smell the evergreens. He saw streams by the roadside. He listened to "All Time Low," by Jon Bellion. The song fascinated Drew. The lyrics did not seem to match the music. The song was about heartbreak, but the tempo and the beat were energetic and strong. The song made Drew feel uneasy, and it fit his mood perfectly. Drew watched the forest pass outside his car window, and he thought about quitting football. He could bury his thoughts and feelings for a little while, but they always surfaced, especially at times, like now, when Drew had a chance to relax.

He should feel calm and peaceful, but he felt anxious and confused. The feeling reminded Drew of the headaches that he suffered after his concussion. The pain was always there. Sometimes it was dull, and he almost forgot about it. At other times the pain was intense, and the hurt caught Drew off guard. *I got better because I accepted that I was hurt, and I took care of myself,* thought Drew. Drew knew that he could not run and hide in the mountains forever. He knew that he was going to have to face reality and accept that his football career was over. Drew also knew that he would have to face his friends. Whether he was ready or not, Drew was returning to Hingham, and he was going to have to face his problems. *But how?* he asked himself. Drew felt the beat of the drums in his headphones, and it gave him a jolt of courage.

Drew spent the next few weeks working as a parking attendant at Sandy Beach in nearby Cohasset. It was the easiest job ever created. Drew sat at the entrance to the parking lot in a beach chair under a giant umbrella. Cars would pull up to him, and he would check that they had a parking sticker. If the car had a little, yellow sticker on the bottom left side of the windshield, then Drew waved them in. If the car did not have a sticker, then Drew waved them in anyway, and he used a walkie talkie to tell his manager about it. Drew could have used the time to do his summer reading, but he took it easy and settled into a nice summer routine. He worked; he went for a run; he watched the Red Sox with his Dad. The biggest decision of his day was whether he should drink an Arnold Palmer or a Root Beer Float while he watched the baseball game. Drew didn't see very much of his friends because everybody traveled so much in the summer. However, Drew never felt lonely because there were lots of new people to meet at Sandy Beach. Drew had escaped to the mountains, and now he escaped to the beach. His anxiety returned once in a while, but he procrastinated. Drew got good at procrastinating. *You don't need to worry about that yet,* he told himself.

In the second week of August, reality finally caught up with Drew. His friends returned to Hingham, and Drew's phone was full of texts about the freshman football team's first meeting. With each text message Drew's anxiety intensified. He tried to ignore his friends, but his headaches returned, and his summer tan could not hide the worry on his face. The night of the meeting came, and Drew stayed home and watched the Red Sox on TV. Late in the game Drew's doorbell rang. Brendan, Scott, and Troy were outside. Drew opened the door.

"Where were you?" asked Scott.

"Hey guys," said Drew. "Come in."

The boys walked into the Hennings' living room. Mr. Hennings was there. He greeted the boys and excused himself.

After he left, Scott said, "What's up with you, Drew? You don't answer our texts, and you didn't go to the meeting. What's going on?"

Drew looked at the floor, and he said, "I'm not going to play football this year. I'm sorry guys."

"What?" said Scott.

Troy said, "Drew, you love football. What's going on?"

"I can't get hurt like that again," said Drew.

Brendan was too stunned to speak.

Troy finally said, "I get it."

"You're the best player on our team. What are we gonna do?" asked Scott.

"Whoa, Scott. We all thought that Drew was paralyzed that night," said Brendan.

"That was scary," said Troy.

"Is there any way that we can get you to change your mind?" asked Scott.

Don't cry. Breathe, thought Drew. Drew couldn't look at them. "No," he said.

No one knew what to say next. Troy said, "I don't blame you, Drew. After you took that hit, you weren't yourself for a long time. I wouldn't want to risk that again either," said Troy.

Drew looked up. "Thanks," he said.

"We're still your friends," said Brendan.

"Yeah," said Scott.

"But—" said Troy. "You're the team leader. Why didn't you tell us sooner?"

Drew's head was down, and he said nothing.

"Whoever takes your place could have used some extra time to get ready," said Scott.

Drew said nothing.

"You're definitely not changing your mind? You're sure?" asked Scott.

Drew couldn't look at them, but he nodded.

Troy finally said, "We'll miss you, man."

"Yeah," said Brendan.

Drew looked up, "Me too," he said.

"We'll see you at school," said Scott.

"Yeah," said Drew.

The boys said their goodbyes and left. When they were gone, Drew went upstairs to bed. *I'm glad that's over,* he thought. There was a part of him that felt proud. Drew had been dreading that conversation for a long time, and he did it. However, it didn't exactly go smoothly. He could not stop thinking about Troy's question: "Why didn't you tell us sooner?" Troy had been supportive, and he was right to say what he said. Drew replayed the conversation over and over again in his mind. *Should I have told them what I've been through? Could I have told them?* he wondered. At first Drew felt embarrassed and ashamed.

He threw the covers off of his body. Later, Drew felt angry. *When was I supposed to tell them? They didn't want to talk about football. Maybe if they hadn't acted like such a bunch of crybabies about losing the game, then I could have told them sooner?* he thought. Drew clenched his fists and then pulled at his hair. *When I came back to school, did any of them ask how I was doing? Did any of them visit? I guess that they were too busy playing video games,* he thought. Drew could not lie still. Eventually Drew's anger wore him down. Before he fell asleep one of the last things that he remembered thinking was: *No football, no friends, now what do I do?*

As the Dog Days of Summer began, Drew still had trouble sleeping. He fought to stay awake at work. Drew didn't feel like eating, and he took long naps in the late afternoons. Drew still didn't do any of his summer reading. He brought the book, *the curious incident of the dog in the nighttime*, with him to work, but trying to read it was like taking a sleeping pill. The only time that Drew felt like himself was when he went for a run. In the third week of August, when his friends reported to preseason workouts, Drew felt worse than ever. Mom and Dad were worried, and they called Drew's doctor. One night Drew saw Mom filling out a giant packet that said "Developmental-Behavioral Pediatrics" at the top of it. The old Drew would have found out what his Mom was up to and argued with her until he convinced her that he was ok. Instead Drew went upstairs to bed.

Freshman Orientation took place on the Thursday before Labor Day weekend. Drew dragged himself out of bed and managed to make himself look presentable before the school bus arrived. The bus ride was hot and sweaty. When Drew arrived at the high school, he and the rest of the ninth grade were directed to the auditorium where they watched a video about life at Hingham High School and listened to speeches from the Principal, a Guidance Counselor, and the President of the Student Council. Afterwards, the students walked through their entire schedules, and they met with each of their teachers for ten minutes. There were countless upperclassmen volunteers in the hallways to help them find their way through the unfamiliar halls of the school. The school was sweltering. Drew's friends seemed to know everyone wearing a Hingham Football t-shirt.

A massive varsity football player shouted, "What's up seven-five!"

"Hey, seven-six!" Scott said. "That's Jake. He's a junior. Sometimes I have to block him in positional drills."

"He's a junior?" Drew asked. "In high school or college?"

"He's a beast," said Scott, and he smiled.

Just then another upperclassman football player greeted them "Callahan! You're not making any more catches on me today!"

Troy smiled, and he said to Drew, "I play against the varsity defensive backs during passing drills."

Drew looked at the floor and said, "Cool." All of Drew's friends talked non-stop about football. Drew remained silent. Orientation ended after lunch. Brendan, Troy, and Scott stayed on campus for football practice. Drew said a quick goodbye and walked alone towards the busses. The bus was carrying only the freshman class, and there were plenty of empty seats. Drew sat alone and looked out the window. When he got home, he said nothing to his parents and went right to his room.

Labor Day Weekend arrived, and, like always, Drew's family went to Sandy Beach with their friends. Drew found out that the freshman football team would have a scrimmage on Saturday morning. To take his mind off of missing the scrimmage, Drew worked checking parking passes, and he read his book. In the afternoon his friends arrived. Drew recognized the cars as soon as they turned into the entrance. He tried to hide his book, but Brendan called out, "I didn't know you could read!"

"Will you do my summer reading too?" asked Scott.

Drew said, "I'll be done in a half an hour. I'll see you guys on the beach." He waved the cars through.

Drew joined everyone on the sand and asked his friends about the scrimmage.

"I think that we did alright, but the passing game is in rough shape," said Scott.

"It's hard to tell when we do ten plays on offense and then ten plays on defense," said Brendan.

"And all of the series start at the fifty-yard line," added Troy.

Listening to the football talk was bittersweet for Drew. *I don't want them to do too well,* thought Drew.

"Brendan looked good running the ball. That's the most important thing. The timing is off on the passes, but we'll figure it out," said Troy.

"It's going to be so much fun when we do. Drew, the offense is wide open. We spread out the defense with at least four receivers. We run wide; we run option, and when the defense gets tired, we throw the ball to Troy!" said Brendan.

"Cool," said Drew.

"We try to throw the ball," said Troy. "The QB's timing is off, and his arm strength isn't great, but that's what practice is for, right?"

Drew smiled. *I shouldn't have done that,* he thought.

"I'm so glad that the preseason is over. It's gonna be nice to only practice once a day," said Brendan.

Drew looked away towards the ocean. *What a crybaby! I would kill to play again!* he thought.

The boys started playing catch in the water, and Drew felt almost normal. When they were done, they dried off by playing Spikeball on the hot sand. For dinner the Hennings and their friends had pizza delivered to the beach. There was still an hour of daylight left. After they had eaten, Dad played catch with Drew. Mike Hennings' best friend, Jack, joined them.

"You throw pretty well for a former offensive tackle," Dad said.

"Our coaches at Brown made a mistake. I should have been a tight end," said Jack.

"Were you guys roommates all four years?" asked Drew.

"Yes," said Dad.

"Sorry about that, Uncle Jack," said Drew.

"I appreciate that, Drew, but you've had to live with him for a lot longer than I did. Do you think that you can hang in there for four more years?" asked Jack.

They laughed.

Jack continued, "Drew, your Dad was telling me that you have a community service requirement at the high school."

"Yeah," said Drew. "The Guidance Counselors at Orientation told us that it was forty hours."

"Do you would want to work with me?" asked Jack.

"Doing what?" asked Drew.

"You know that I'm a referee. Sometimes on Saturdays I officiate the flag football league for elementary school kids. I usually work a varsity game on Friday nights and Youth Football on Sundays. When I work with the younger kids, I could be the brain, and you could be the brawn," said Jack.

"You want me to ref with you?" said Drew.

"I'd be grateful for the help. As the season goes on, my legs get pretty sore," said Jack.

"Would I have to wear a striped shirt and throw flags?" asked Drew.

"When we work with the younger kids, we don't throw many flags," said Jack. "We help keep the kids safe and keep the games fair. Don't worry about equipment. I have a lot of extra gear that you could borrow."

"That's very nice of you, Uncle Jack. It's just—I don't know if reffing is really my thing. Someone might see me," said Drew.

Dad jumped into the conversation, and he said, "Drew, you're helping little kids. No one is going to give you a hard time about that. Think of it this—"

"Wanna bet?" said Drew. *First I can't play football, and now this? Can it get any worse?* Drew wondered.

"Jack's trying to do you favor. You don't need to be a wise guy," said Dad.

"Sorry, Uncle Jack," said Drew.

"Apology accepted," said Jack.

Dad went on, "You get community service hours, and you stay around the game you love," said Dad.

So that's what this is about, thought Drew. "Dad, I get it. Thank you. But I can watch football on TV any day of the week," said Drew.

"But do you get paid to watch games like I do?" asked Jack. "Maybe we could work something out where you donate some of your time, and you get paid for the rest," said Jack. "Last year I think that we got thirty-five dollars for every flag football game that we worked," said Jack.

"How many games do you ref?" asked Drew.

"There are usually four of them, grades two through five. I usually work two or three," said Jack.

"So you get paid one hundred and five dollars to watch little kids play flag football for three hours?" asked Drew.

"How much are they paying you to check beach stickers?" asked Dad.

"I get ten dollars an hour," said Drew.

"So on a good day you make between sixty and eighty?" asked Dad.

"Something like that," said Drew.

"So you could make that much in half the time and earn community service hours and be around football and hang out with Uncle Jack," said Dad.

Drew was startled by his Dad's reasoning. He was silent for a moment. *I could save up and buy a new snowboard,* he thought. *Or new equipment for lax or video games,* Drew thought. Money meant freedom, and freedom made Drew smile.

Dad saw his opportunity. "I remember you bugging mom and me about a new snowboard. If you had your own money, then it would be pretty hard for us to stand in your way," he said.

"You're going to be driving in two years, Drew. It might be a good idea to start saving up for a car," said Jack.

"That's a good point," Drew said to himself. *Did I just say that out loud?* he thought.

"I could set this up for you," said Jack. "Are you in?"

"Yeah, I'm in," said Drew. Drew noticed that his father was giving him a stern look. "Oh, yeah. Thanks, Uncle Jack," said Drew.

"You're welcome," said Jack. Then Jack threw Drew a perfect spiral, but Jack threw the ball underhand. Drew gave Jack a puzzled look.

"Referees always throw the ball underhand," said Jack.

Drew nodded. He turned back to see what his friends were doing. They had started another game of Spikeball. Drew rolled

1

his eyes. *They seem to be getting along just fine without me,* he thought. He shook his head. *Or they saw me talking with my Dad, and they didn't want to interrupt. Maybe I'll try to get in on the next game.* Drew kept throwing the football with Jack and his Dad until it was too dark to see.

Chapter 7
TEEN REF

The next weekend Drew was jolted awake by his alarm. He turned it off and crawled slowly out of bed. He sat on the edge of his bed with his head in his hands. *Why did I agree to do this?* Drew thought. It was eight a.m. on a Saturday. It had taken him the entire week to adjust his sleep schedule to the school day, and Drew was very excited to be able to sleep past 6:30 a.m. The school rule was that each class could only give thirty minutes of homework per night, but Drew did not believe that the teachers were following it. Drew had a Study Hall during E period, the fifth period of the day, and although he did his homework, he still had at least two hours of work to do when he got home. *I'm not thinking about homework again until Sunday night,* he decided. Drew put on some workout gear and went downstairs for breakfast. Mom and Dad had a plate ready for him, "Jack's picking you up at 8:45am," said his Dad.

"I put two sports drinks and a protein bar on the counter for you. You're going to need them today. It's going to be another hot one," said his Mom.

"Thanks," said Drew. He ate and looked at the stack of mail on the table.

"Anything for me in there?"

"No," said Mom. She did not look at Drew when she spoke.

"Oh," said Drew.

"I used to love to open mail from recruiters too," said Dad. "But you can't look back. Are you excited to work with Jack today?"

"I'm tired," said Drew.

"It was a tough week, but you can rest at the beach this afternoon," said Mom.

Drew had finished breakfast and was brushing his teeth when Jack arrived. Drew raced downstairs, stuffed the drinks into his sports bag, put his running shoes on without tying the laces and ran out to the driveway.

"Hi, Uncle Jack!" said Drew.

"Throw your bag in the trunk. It's open," said Uncle Jack.

Drew did as he was told, and Dad came out to talk to Jack.

"It's going to be another hot one. We'll see you at Sandy Beach for lunch?"

"We'll be there," said Jack.

"We will?" said Drew.

"Don't worry. We'll pack your stuff for you. I think that after running around on the turf for a few hours you're going to want to jump in the ocean," said Dad.

"We'll see you there. Thanks, Dad!" said Drew, and they drove off.

As they were turning out of the neighborhood, Jack said, "It's 8:40am. We've got to hustle," said Jack.

"Why?" Drew asked. "The games are at Hingham High, and they don't start until 9 a.m."

"The officials always get there early," said Jack. Then he said, "Your gear is in the back seat."

Drew turned and saw a gift-wrapped box. "What's this?" he asked.

"Open it," said Jack.

Drew tore open the wrapping paper and opened the box. There was a black and white striped referee shirt, a fitted black referee hat, two whistles, and a yellow flag.

I actually have to wear this stuff, Drew thought. Drew had a sinking feeling in his stomach. He took a deep breath and tried to think on the bright side: *Maybe this will be a great Halloween costume someday,* he thought. He remembered his manners and said, "Thanks, Jack."

"None of my old stuff was going to fit you. You're just not built like a lineman. I ordered it online. Your dad helped me with the sizes. I have a premium membership so the stuff shipped fast," said Jack.

Drew could tell that Jack really wanted him to like the presents. He tried on the hat and started shaping the brim, "You nailed it, Uncle Jack. It fits perfectly."

"Great. I was hoping that we'd get that right. I had your Dad do some undercover reconnaissance for me," said Jack.

"Say what now?" said Drew.

"I had your Dad find an old hat of yours and tell me what size it was," said Jack.

"Gotcha," said Drew. Next he looked at the two whistles. One had a lanyard that went around his neck. The other was a finger whistle that officials wore like a big ring on their index and middle fingers.

Jack said, "You always want to wear two whistles in a game, just in case one breaks. I didn't know which kind you would like the best, so I got one of each."

"Cool," said Drew. "Which kind do you use?"

"The veteran officials all use whistles that hang around their necks. They argue that it's the best way to go because you have to grab the whistle and raise it to your mouth before you make any sound. The veterans believe that this gives you more time to think so that you don't make a mistake, or make *the* mistake," said Jack.

"What is *the* mistake?" Drew asked.

"It's called an inadvertent whistle. It's when an official blows the whistle by mistake and stops the game for no reason. It is the Cardinal Sin of officiating. I remember that in my first year of officiating, I was working a freshman game in North Quincy. The team hadn't won a game for the entire year. A pass got batted in the air, and the North Quincy cornerback intercepted it with nothing but green grass and the team's first win in front of him. I blew an inadvertent whistle. As soon as the pass got tipped, I thought, *It's going to be incomplete*, and I blew the whistle. That was fifteen years ago, and I still feel bad about it."

"Whoa. No inadvertent whistles. Got it," said Drew. "So what do I do with the finger whistle?"

"Most of the officials on our board don't use them, but I really like them. I'm not always putting it down and picking it back up. I feel that the whistle on your finger is more efficient. It's right there when you need it. You don't have to fumble around for it when you're under pressure to make a big call. Yeah, the easier access might put me in more danger of blowing an inadvertent whistle, but if I'm focused on the game, then I'm not going to make that mistake. Anyway, I'll be interested to see which one you like better," said Jack.

"I think that I'll just copy you today and see how it goes," said Drew. "Thanks again for all of this gear," said Drew.

"You're welcome," said Jack as he pulled into the high school parking lot. He parked the car and turned off the engine. "Drew, you know that you're like the son I never had. Every once in a while I'm going to buy you some stuff, and you're going to have to deal with it," said Jack.

"I can handle that," said Drew. *What is with this guy right now? He is way too fired up about reffing,* Drew thought. "Jack?"

"Yeah?"

"I can tell that you really love this. Why do you like reffing so much?"

"Well, I think that there are three reasons. I think that the first two reasons are that Mary and I don't have any children of our own, and the other reason is that even though I'm too old to play football, I still love it. When I officiate, I get to be around kids and stay connected to football," said Jack.

"Cool," said Drew. "What's the third reason?"

"Work," said Jack. "I would love to coach, but my law firm would never let me leave early every afternoon in the fall. Officiating is great because you don't have to be there for all of the practices, but you still get to watch the games. The Firm encourages me because they like it when the lawyers do something outside of work to serve the community."

"So it's like a hobby, but you get to help people?" asked Drew.

"Yes," said Jack.

"I just thought that we were getting paid to watch a football game," said Drew.

"Drew, one thing that football has taught me about life is that if you want to be successful, then you have to be selfless, and you have to have a clear purpose," said Jack. "For example, why did you play quarterback?"

"So that I could score touchdowns and help our team win games," said Drew.

"Why did you mention helping your teammates last?" asked Jack. "Your father and I wanted to make great plays and win too. We had great college careers because we were friends, and we played for each other. That made each of us better."

"I wanted to help my friends too," said Drew. "What does this have to do with being a ref?"

"It doesn't matter if you're a player, a coach, or an official. Like I said before, if you want to be good at football, then you have to be selfless and have a clear purpose. We both liked playing football, and it taught both of us a lot about ourselves and about life. As officials we've got to pay that forward, and we can if we work together and support each other. If you go out on the field to watch a game and get paid, then you're not going to be a very good ref," said Jack.

"But the players and the coaches and the fans don't see it that way," said Drew. "The only time I ever notice referees is when they're getting yelled at."

"You take the good with the bad. Sometimes we make bad calls, and the coaches get mad at us. I can't really blame them. It's an emotional game. I was intense when I played too. The weird thing about officiating football is that if you do your job right, then no one even notices that you're there."

Drew was silent. It was a lot to take in.

"I could talk about this all day, but how about I show you? Are you ready?" asked Jack.

Drew quickly put everything on, and took a look at himself in the car's rearview mirror. *No one knows. All of your friends are playing in a scrimmage down in Plymouth. It's for community service,* he thought.

Jack said, "You look great, but I don't think that today's games are televised."

"Right. Sorry," said Drew. *How long was I looking at myself?* he thought. Drew opened the door and stepped out of the car.

Jack said, "Your extra whistle is around your neck?"

"Yes," said Drew.

"Put it inside your shirt so it doesn't bounce around and hit you in the face," said Jack.

"Will do," said Drew.

"Where's your flag?" asked Jack.

"In my pocket," said Drew. He took out the flag. It looked like a little, yellow ghost. The head of the ghost was filled with little beads, and to Drew it felt like a hacky sack.

"Don't keep the flag in your pocket. Keep it in the waistband of your shorts," said Jack.

"Why?" asked Drew.

"If you reach into your pocket and start digging around for your flag, then the coaches are going to notice. If you decide not to throw it, then they are going to ask you why you changed your mind. Sometimes they forget to ask politely. Anyway, we're not throwing flags today because these guys are little. We'll just blow the whistle and correct them," said Jack.

"Got it," said Drew. As he walked through the parking lot, he pulled the hat down low on his forehead. Jack and Drew walked onto the turf, and they were hit by a wall of heat. There were six other officials already standing in the middle of the field.

"Hey Jack! Is this the kid that you were talking to us about?" asked a tall, thin old man with a mop of silver hair under his faded black referee's hat. Drew noticed that the man was already beginning to sweat through the hat.

Jack shook the old man's hand and said, "Good to see you, John. This is Drew. He's a freshman here at Hingham High School, and he was the quarterback of the eighth grade team last year. He's here to help us out and do some community service."

"Hi," said Drew. He raised his hand to say hello and quickly dropped it.

"You were the quarterback?" asked John.

"Yes," said Drew.

"I was the referee for your Super Bowl game," said John.

Drew took a good look at John and decided that he looked vaguely familiar.

"That was a heck of a game. You played great," said John. John now spoke to the entire circle of officials, "This kid was the best athlete on the field. Remember the story that I told you guys at the end-of-the-year banquet, the story about the forty-eight-yard Quarterback Sneak for a touchdown? This is the kid who did it. In all of my years of officiating football, I have never seen a play like that. I almost blew my whistle when you broke the first tackle. I'm really glad that I didn't. What a run you made!"

Drew felt like he was a star recruit again, and he was the center of attention. He smiled. "Thanks," he said. Drew looked around the circle, but it wasn't private school coaches smiling back at him, it was a bunch of guys wearing black and white "zebra" stripes. *This is weird,* he thought. Drew recovered from the shock and said, "That would have been an inadvertent whistle, right?"

John nodded and smiled, "That's right."

"Jack was giving me some advice on the drive over here," said Drew.

"I learned it all from you, John," Jack said.

"That's what I'm afraid of," said John. The officials laughed. "Gentleman, I have great news. This kid can run, and that will be a big help for all of us in this heat. Jack, I know we talked about Drew staying with you for the entire morning, but can we rotate him through each group? He can start with you, of course."

"Is that alright with you, Drew?" asked Jack.

"Sure. Whatever you guys need," said Drew. Drew didn't mean what he said, and his stomach turned when he said it. *Of course I only want to work with Jack: I don't know any of you, and I have no idea what I'm doing!* he thought. *All right, chill out, Drew. Be a team player. You'll work your first game with Jack, and he'll teach you everything that you need to know.*

"Drew, the kids play from sideline to sideline, and the field is only twenty-five yards wide. Why don't you and Jack start on the field near the scoreboard, and you can rotate from there? We made pairs right before you arrived. We'll keep an older official with a younger official for every game. Old guys, stay put. Young guys, rotate. When you work with Drew, you will get a little rest because, believe me, this kid's got wheels. Are there any questions?"

No one said anything.

"Let's go!" said John.

Drew jogged with Jack to their quarter of the field. As soon as they got there, Jack took over.

"Kindergartners and First Graders, everyone circle up on me!" said Jack.

The players did as they were told.

"Boys and girls, please take a knee," said Jack.

The players struggled to follow Jack's instruction, but he didn't miss a beat. "1-2-3, eyes on me! Just do what I do, ok?" Jack bent down and rested his right knee on the turf. Drew took the initiative and did the same thing. All of the players followed.

When they were all settled, one of the little boys said, "The ground is too hot."

Drew jumped in, "It is really hot today. You can sit criss-cross-applesauce if you want to, ok? That way your skin won't touch the turf."

"Ok," said the little boy.

Jack looked at Drew and smiled. Then he said, "My name's Jack, and this is Drew, and we're your officials today."

"Hi!" said the kids. Many of them waved. Drew tried to look serious, but he smiled.

Jack said, "I see that we have the Green Bay Packers and the Denver Broncos here today. I think that it's going to be a great game, don't you Drew?"

"Yes, sir," said Drew.

Jack looked to the coaches who were standing behind their teams and said, "Who is the visiting team today?"

One of the coaches said, "The Packers are the visitors."

"Alright, coach. Do you have a captain who wants to call the coin toss?"

"Max, why don't you do it?" A stocky boy with tussled red hair stood up.

"Alright, Max!" said Jack. "Come right over here, and stand beside me. Does everyone know Max?"

There was a chorus "yeah" and "no."

"Why don't you wave to everyone ok, Max?" Jack waited. "Ok, Max. The coin toss decides who gets the ball first. Do you want the ball first?"

Max nodded.

"Coach, do you want Max to want the ball first?" asked Jack.

"Yes, please," said the coach.

"Excellent," said Jack. Next, Jack took a quarter from his pocket and showed it to Max. He showed him which side was Heads and which side was Tails. "Max, before I flip this coin, I want you to guess what's going to happen. Is it going to land on Heads, or is it going to land on Tails?"

"Heads," said Max.

"Drew, I heard Heads. Did you hear Heads?" asked Jack.

"I heard Heads," said Drew.

Jack flipped the coin, and it landed on the turf. He picked it up and showed it to Max and asked him what side it was.

"Heads," said Max.

"That's right," said Jack. "You've won. You told me that you want to have the ball first. Is that right?"

"Yes," said Max.

"Coaches, normally we'd ask which of you wants which side, but given that there is no wind, no shade, and no scoreboard, maybe the best thing to do is just keep them where they are?"

The coaches agreed.

"Alright, Packers you are going to come with me. Broncos, you are going to go with Drew. We're going to kick this ball off and play some football!" said Jack.

The kids cheered. Jack turned to Drew and said, "Line them up on the hash marks. Put the ball on a tee a few yards in front of them. Tell them to stay put until I blow the whistle. You work on the left side of the field, and I'll work on the right side of the field. Got it?"

"Got it," said Drew. He turned to the players and said, "Broncos, run over here with me!" They followed. Drew found it surprisingly difficult to get the kids to line up and stand still. "Wait for Jack to blow his whistle, and then you can kick the ball!" He said. When he finally jogged to the sideline, Drew was already sweating. As soon as Drew turned around, Jack blew his whistle, and the game began. The opening kickoff bounced low along the ground. It was scooped up by a little girl on the Packers, and she ran with the ball for twenty yards until one of the Broncos took her flag.

"Packers, line up across the field right here. Coach, pick your quarterback and tell her or him what to do. Broncos, take one big step away from the other team, and line up across the field. Coach, tell them who is guarding whom!" Jack looked at Drew and said, "If the ball carrier runs to your side, then sound the whistle once very loudly when the play is over. Throw the ball to me in the middle of the field. If the play comes to my side, then run to the middle of the field to catch the ball, and put it down on the ground. We call this 'spotting the ball.' Got it?"

"Got it," said Drew.

On the next play the Packers' quarterback handed the ball off to another little girl who ran the ball wide towards Drew's side of the field. She gained seven yards before a Bronco took her flag. Drew blew his whistle loudly and jogged to the spot. He took the ball and threw it underhand to Jack. The pass was a tight spiral, and it hit Jack right in the hands.

"Nice toss, kid!" said Jack.

Drew smiled.

The Packers tried to run the ball again, but by now the Broncos knew what to do, and the runner did not get very far.

"It's going to be third down, Jack," said Drew.

"No downs. The offense just keeps going until they score, and then we switch," said Jack.

"Got it," said Drew.

It took the Packers five more plays to score, and it was Max who ran the ball into the end zone. Drew jogged to the goal line and raised his hands above his head to signal for a touchdown. "Way to go, Max!" he said.

Drew walked up to him and said, "Can I have the ball so that we can get ready for the next kick off?"

"Here you go, sir" said Max. Max looked at Drew and smiled. Max's joy was infectious.

"Football is fun isn't it?" said Drew.

Max nodded.

"I think so too," said Drew. He smiled, and he and Max bumped knuckles.

Jack and Drew jogged upfield to set up for the kickoff, and Jack said, "I didn't catch you having fun did I?"

Drew looked straight ahead and said, "No, sir."

"Good," said Jack. "I have a quick tip for you about spotting the ball: after you place the ball on the turf, try not to turn your back on the players. You might miss something. Back peddle just like you used to when you played safety."

"Got it," said Drew.

The Broncos received the kickoff and began their march down the field. Drew enjoyed interacting with the players. "Throw that ball to me, big man," he said at the end of one play. Drew caught the ball and said, "Thata boy!"

As the Broncos moved closer to a touchdown, Drew found a rhythm. He was only blowing the whistle when the play came to his side. He was spotting the ball accurately, and he wasn't turning his back on the players. Drew threw another underhand spiral to Jack, and Jack said, "We haven't dropped a pass yet. Have you ever had a completion percentage that high?"

"I know that you haven't," said Drew.

"A wise guy, huh? You're just like your Dad. It's a good thing I never had to block for you. I might have missed an assignment or two," Jack said with a smile.

Drew smiled back. On the next play, a Broncos player committed a false start, and Drew blew his whistle.

Jack said to the Broncos, "Don't forget to wait for the quarterback to start the play, ok? Try again."

Several plays later the Broncos scored a touchdown, and Drew and Jack jogged down the field together.

Jack said, "Drew, when there's a penalty or a timeout or an injury, blow your whistle at least three times. That is how we tell each other to stop the game."

"One sound stops the play. Three sounds stops the game because something might be wrong," repeated Drew.

"You've got it," said Jack.

Drew put his new lesson to work on the Packers' next drive. After they finally scored, Drew said, "Great throw!" to the little girl who had given him the ball. He and Jack jogged back for the kickoff, and Jack said, "Good work with the whistle."

"Thanks," Drew replied.

When the game ended, each team had scored three touchdowns. The players lined up and shook hands, and many of them came over to Drew and Jack. They thanked them and slapped them five too. As the kids walked off of the field, Jack said, "Are you smiling?"

"No, sir," said Drew.

"Good," said Jack. "For the second grade game, you're going to the next field to work with John. They're going to pass a little bit, so you'll have to run more. Make sure that you get something to drink first."

Drew's bag was on the bench at midfield. He jogged over and chugged his sports drink. It was warm and sweet. He wiped his mouth with the back of his hand and jogged over to John. John quizzed him on what he had learned during his first game. The second game began, and the Patriots played against the Vikings. Drew was surprised at how much better the second grade players were compared to the younger group. On the Vikings' opening drive, the quarterback threw a high pass down the middle of the field. Players from both sides leapt to catch the football, and a Viking made the reception. He turned and raced for the end zone. Drew put his head down and sprinted for the goal line. He raced past the receiver, stopped at the goal line, and looked back just in time to see the receiver caught from behind by a Patriots defender. Drew spotted the ball and waited for John and the other players to jog downfield. The Vikings scored on the next play.

As John and Drew jogged slowly back for the kickoff, John said, "You haven't lost a step since last year, kid. You can fly!"

The compliment was bittersweet. *Yeah,* Drew thought. *And I should be using it at the Plymouth Scrimmage to score touchdowns.*

"Thanks," said Drew.

"But listen: don't race the ball carrier to the end zone. Keep him in front of you, and trail the play."

"Really?" Drew asked.

"Really," John replied. "It's hard to watch the action when you're sprinting, and the players are behind you. Even though you were at the goal line ahead of the runner, you had to run back to spot the ball. If you had been trailing the play, then you would have been at the spot where it ended just two or three steps after the runner. You're a hard working kid, but you have to work smart too."

"Yes, sir," said Drew. He was breathing hard, and he had his hands on his hips. He felt like a quarterback again, and it reminded him of how he used to look and feel when the coach would tell him what play to take to the huddle. Drew hated making mistakes on the football field, and he did not overrun another play for the rest of the half. It was 10:30 am, and the turf was scorching hot. The second graders took a half time break for water and oranges. John and Drew joined the other officials at the bench. While they were drinking waters and sports drinks, John said, "Jack, did you teach Drew how to 'square in' when he's spotting the ball?"

"No," said Jack.

"It's easy, Drew," John explained. "The first thing that you do is trail the play, just like we talked about during the first half. You want to be in a position where you can see as much of the action on the field as possible, and you want to get to the ball quickly when the action stops. However, you don't want to take a curved route to the spot where the play ends, you want to get there and make a crisp, ninety-degree turn towards the middle of the field."

"Like a soldier?" Drew asked.

"Yes. Be controlled, and be confident," said John. "Will you work on that in the second half?"

"No problem," said Drew.

The second half began, and Drew was as good as his word. After the Vikings scored their first touchdown of the second half, Drew said, "That was a great touchdown catch number 9! Well done!"

"Thanks!" she said before she celebrated with her teammates. *This isn't such a bad way to complete my community service hours,* Drew thought. The game ended, and the players thanked John and Drew.

"Are you sure you don't want to stay on this field for the third grade game?" asked John.

"I'll do whatever," Drew replied.

John called over to Kevin, the veteran official on the adjacent field, "Hey, Kevin! I'm going to keep Drew for this game, ok?"

"Not a chance!" Kevin said.

John shrugged. "I tried."

"Thank you," said Drew, and he jogged to the next field for the third grade game. Drew was tired, but he was enjoying the physical and mental challenge of working with older players. In this game, Kevin and Drew started to count the downs and turn the ball over to the opponent if the offense did not advance at least ten yards. Kevin kept track of the line to gain to earn a new first down, and he taught Drew how officials use signals to count the downs. The signal for first down was a simple index finger in the air. The signal for second down was like making bullhorns with the index and the pinky fingers. Kevin taught Drew that the signal for third down was the same as the sign for "ok." Finally, Drew learned that the signal for fourth down was simply a fist in the air. The first half flew by, but Drew was grateful for a halftime rest. The officials gathered again around the bench at midfield. Drew chugged his sports drink. It tasted like sugary bathwater.

"I'm glad that you brought the kid, Jack," said John after he poured some of his water down the back of his neck. "We need his legs."

The other officials agreed. Jack continued, "We've thrown a lot at him today, but he hasn't missed a beat."

"Thanks," said Drew. "I'm a quarterback—ah— I *was* a quarterback." He stared at the turf. "Anyway, I'm used to thinking when I'm tired and under pressure."

"You're doing great, Drew," said Jack.

Drew gave Jack a sad smile.

"Listen, Jack," said John. "Can we keep Drew around for the fourth game? I know that you were going to leave after this game, but we sure could use his speed and stamina for the last game of the day."

"I promised his Dad I would get him home before lunch," said Jack.

"What if we give him half community service and half pay: two community service hours, and seventy dollars?"

"Really?" Drew said. "Count me in. My parents won't mind."

"Should we text them?" asked Jack.

"No need," said Drew. "Besides, by the time you find your phone, write the message, and send it, the game will be over."

"I meant 'should you text them?' wise guy," said Jack.

"It's fine," said Drew.

"Great," said John.

The next hour and a half flew by. Drew was hot, sweaty, and exhausted. The final game ended with a chorus of "thank you's" from the players. Drew slapped fives with some of the players, and he bumped knuckles with others. He walked off of the field with Jack and John, and Drew folded seventy dollars in cash and put it in his pocket.

"The kid's got talent," said John. "Do you want me to tell the Commissioner about him?"

"Why not?" said Jack.

"We've never had an official who was under eighteen, but—" said John.

"Drew's big; he's fast; he's smart; he understands the game; he's good with the kids. Yes, he's still fourteen, but he's already good at this. With a little training and some practice, he could be—" said Jack.

"You're right, Jack. I'll talk to the Commissioner. Maybe Drew could take the Candidate's Class and work some youth games?" said John.

Drew was looking at both of them with wide eyes.

Jack put his hand on Drew's shoulder, and he said, "Relax, buddy. We'll talk more on the beach." Jack continued talking to John, "It's worth a shot. I'm having lunch with Drew and his family today. His Dad and I played together at Brown. I'll talk to them about it. Can you have the Commissioner call me?"

"Sure thing. A teen ref. And I thought that I had seen it all when I saw Drew run a Quarterback Sneak for a forty-yard touchdown," said John.

"Forty-eight yards," said Drew. They shook hands and walked to their cars.

Chapter 8
THE CANDIDATES' CLASS

When Drew and Jack arrived at Sandy Beach, Drew dropped his bag and shoes, ran for the water, and dove in. He floated for fifteen minutes until the chill of the Atlantic Ocean finally cooled him down. Drew walked back to his parents and Jack and took a seat. It was too hot to towel off. Mom had a sports drink and a large Italian sub waiting for him.

"Drew, tell me about refereeing," said Mom.

"It was good. It was hot. I learned a lot, and I ran a lot," he said between bites. He paused to see if he would be allowed so brief a summary. His mother's silence let Drew know that she expected a report with richer detail. "Oh yeah, I made seventy dollars. He reached into his pocket and extracted a wet wad of bills.

Mom shook her head.

Dad said, "Drew, what are you doing? You could have lost all of your money!"

Drew said, "I'll just leave it out to dry like this." He laid the bills on top of the cooler, and they stuck to the plastic.

"Honey, that's going to dry and blow away. Why don't you just give them to me?" said Mom.

"You're a knucklehead," said Dad.

"Didn't you jump into the Mount Washington Hotel pool with your entire wallet in your back pocket?" asked Drew.

"No. It was only a money clip, and it only had my license, a credit card and a little money in it," said Dad.

"My two little boys," said Nancy who looked to Jack for sympathy.

Jack laughed.

"Drew, I was telling your folks what a great job you did out there today. I also told them that John is going to ask the Commissioner if you can join our board," said Jack.

"What's a board anyway?" asked Drew.

"It's the group of football officials who work games in this part of the state, the Eastern Massachusetts Association of Football Officials, E.M.A.F.O," said Jack.

"Isn't that kind of a long name?" asked Drew.

"I guess it is," said Jack.

"Is the Commissioner like the boss of referees?" asked Drew.

"Yes. He assigns us games, and he evaluates us. If coaches complain about us, then the Commissioner finds out what happened and tries to solve the problem."

"Oh," said Drew.

"I don't know what the rules are about teenagers becoming football referees, but John wants to tell the Commissioner about you and see what he says," Jack said.

"Cool. Thanks," said Drew.

"Is that something that you might be interested in?" asked Mom.

Drew looked around to make sure that none of his friends were walking onto the beach. "I guess so," he said.

"Jack was telling us about the Candidates' Class, the class that new officials have to take to learn the rules," said Dad.

"You had to take a whole class to learn the football rules?" asked Drew.

"Yes," said Jack. "The rulebook is pretty big. That's why you have to take a class," said Jack.

"How big is the rulebook?" Drew asked.

"It's about two hundred pages long," said Jack.

"What!"

"It's not too much if you spread it out over the whole season," said Dad.

"The class lasts ten weeks, and each week you learn a new rule. The classes are usually slide show presentations about a rule, practice problems, and watching game film. Sometimes the teachers are college referees, and they always tell great stories. I learn the most from the films and the storytelling," said Jack.

Drew looked over his shoulder. *Are any of my friends coming? I don't want them to hear any of this,* he thought.

"When is the class?" asked Mom.

"The classes are from seven p.m. to nine p.m., and they are at Whitman-Hanson Regional High School," said Jack.

"He's not doing anything after school, but how would we get him there, Mike?" asked Mom.

"I can take him," Jack said.

"Jack, you've done so much already. We would never ask you to—"

"It's no trouble, really. The referees have a weekly meeting at the same time in the lecture hall right next door to where Drew would be. I'm going anyway. I could pick him up at your house and have him back before ten p.m.," said Jack.

"That's really generous. Thanks, Jack," said Dad. "What do you think about this, Drew?"

"Ahhh. I don't know," said Drew. "It sounds weird but cool."

"That's an accurate summary, Drew," said Jack. He turned to Dad. "Maybe we should give the kid a break. He's had enough refereeing for one day. Drew, I'll wait to hear from the Commissioner, and I'll call your folks."

"Thanks, Uncle Jack," said Drew. He took a deep breath and leaned back in his beach chair.

"Once we have all of the information, then we can sit down and talk about it," said Mom.

"Sounds good," said Drew. The grown-ups changed the topic and continued to talk, but Drew fell asleep. He was awakened by ice cold water pouring down his chest.

"Ahhh! What the—" said Drew. He fell sideways out of his chair, scrambled to his feet, and began to run away. When he had retreated to a safe distance, he looked back to see Troy, Scott, and Brendan doubled over with laughter. Drew's parents were laughing too. Shortly afterwards, the boys were throwing a football in the water.

Scott asked Drew, "So what have you been up to this weekend?"

Drew said, "I did some community service over at the school. How did the scrimmage go?"

The boys told Drew all about the scrimmage. The offense had played much better, and the star running back for Plymouth South had dislocated his wrist. The boys each took turns trying to show Drew what the injury looked like. Drew asked them as many questions about the scrimmage as he could think of. *Please don't ask me what I did for community service. Please don't ask me what I did for community service,* he thought.

"I wish that I could have been there," said Drew.

"We do too, buddy. Believe me," said Troy. The words were bittersweet for Drew. *At least they are not making fun of me for being a ref,* he thought.

After they had cooled down, the boys returned to the sand and started up a game of Spikeball. After the game Drew sat on his towel and stared at the waves. The rhythm of the break helped him think. *If the guys find out that I help out little kids during flag football, then it won't be a big deal. But ref class? Studying a rule-book? Doing practice problems? I'll be a joke. Forever,* he thought. Drew remembered Max, the kindergartener on the Packers, smiling at him and bumping knuckles. Drew remembered what Jack had told him, "Pay it forward." *I've got nothing else to do, and I could use the money,* he thought. When his parents called him over to help pack up, Drew still wasn't ready to decide.

On Sunday afternoon, Mom, Dad, Drew, and Libby watched the Patriots play the Miami Dolphins, and they talked about Drew becoming a referee.

"I talked to Jack, and he said the Commissioner wants to meet you. He wants you to come to the meeting on Thursday and work the youth football Jamboree on Sunday in Norwell. The Jamboree is a teaching clinic for new officials. The Commissioner says that you're too young to work high school games, but if you are truly as good as John told him that you were, then you could work flag games and youth football for the rest of the season. You would earn as many community service hours as you want, and you could make a little money too," said Dad.

Drew didn't take his eyes off of the TV. "Cool," he said.

"Is it something that interests you?" Mom asked.

"You'll look so cute in zebra stripes that Callie will fall madly in love with you," said Libby.

Drew threw popcorn at her.

"Libby, that's not helping," said Dad.

"I don't think that I want to be a referee. Can you tell Jack thanks but no thanks, Dad?" said Drew.

"Of course I could, but are you sure? You could be really good at this," said Dad.

"How do you know? Jack probably wants me to be a football ref because they're all, like, a million years old," said Drew.

"Drew, you don't have to officiate football if you don't want to, but what will you do this fall?" asked Mom.

"I don't know," Drew said.

"You have to do something," Dad said.

"I agree," said Mom. "You can't just nap all afternoon, wake up, go through the motions of doing your homework, eat dinner, and go back to bed."

"I don't know, Mom!" said Drew.

"Drew, we just want you to be happy, and when you were working with those kids on Saturday morning, it was the happiest I have seen you since July," said Dad.

"You saw me? How did you—" said Drew.

"Your father and I dropped by to see the end of the game that you worked with Jack," said Mom.

"You spied on me! Mom! That's—I can't believe you—Why—" Drew took a deep breath. "I was working with first graders. I'm not in first grade," he said.

"We should have asked you first. Sorry about that," said Dad.

"It's embarrassing!" said Drew.

"Are you embarrassed to be a referee, or are you embarrassed that we came to watch you?" asked Mom.

"Both!" said Drew.

"Why?" asked Dad.

"Because!" said Drew.

"Because why?" asked Dad.

"I don't know. It's just embarrassing, alright?" said Drew.

"I know what I saw," said Mom. "When you were helping those kids, you looked happy, and you looked like a strong, confident leader. I haven't seen that since before you got hurt."

"You still love football. You like working with kids, and you're good at it. What's there to be embarrassed about?" asked Dad.

"I'm going to be a joke," said Drew.

"People might laugh, and it might take them some time to get used to you being a football referee—" said Dad.

"Oh, they'll laugh," said Libby. Mom silenced Libby with a single look.

"Drew, think about why your friends like you," said Dad.

"Because I was the quarterback," said Drew.

"Are you sure about that?" asked Dad.

Mom jumped in, "How did you act when you were the quarterback?"

"I was confident," said Drew.

"And happy and funny and brave," said Mom. "Those things about you don't go away just because you stop wearing a football uniform."

"Yeah they do," said Drew.

"No, they don't," said Dad. "Did I become a complete loser after I stopped playing college football? Don't answer that, Mom."

Drew smiled.

"Drew, yesterday your mom and I watched you work with those kids, and we think that, maybe, you may have found a part of yourself that was lost," said Dad.

"Go do what you like to do and what you're good at, and try to use your talents to help people. I know that when I do that, I feel happy and confident. I think that you might find the same thing," said Mom.

"People like to be around happy and confident people. Your friends will come around," said Dad.

"I don't know," said Drew.

"You don't have to know," said Mom. "Just try it. Go to the meeting and try the Jamboree. If you have fun, then keep going. If it doesn't make you happy, then move on."

"And you guys won't give me a hard time if I stop after the Jamboree?"

"Promise," said Dad.

"Promise," said Mom.

"I'm your little sister. It's my job to give you a hard time," said Libby.

Drew threw more popcorn at her.

"Ok," said Drew. "I'll try it."

On the following Thursday, Jack picked up Drew at 6:15p.m. The Candidates' Classes were at Whitman-Hanson Regional High School, and it took about thirty minutes of back-road driving to get there. They finally reached the school, went inside the gymnasium entrance, and climbed the stairs to the second floor. They walked down a dimly lit hallway with red lockers on one side and beige lockers on the other. Jack and Drew stopped outside a two level lecture hall with a massive projector screen. It was the perfect setting for presentation, discussion, and film study.

There was a desk outside the lecture hall, and all of the officials had to sign in and take a worksheet of case plays, football word problems that the officials had to solve. Usually the candidates met in an adjacent classroom. Jack directed Drew into the classroom and introduced him to Brian, the teacher.

"He officiated in the Ivy League before he retired. He worked a few of the games that your father and I played in," said Jack.

"Whoa," said Drew.

"He's also got great stories about Harvard vs. Yale games," said Jack.

"When are you and Dad going to take me to one of those?" asked Drew.

"Never," said Jack.

Drew smiled. After he was introduced to the teacher, Drew took a seat, and Jack joined the veteran officials in the lecture hall. The heat of the day still lingered in the classroom, and everything felt damp. Drew looked around the room and counted eight men and two women. *Awkward*, he thought. Drew smiled and looked for a seat. The other candidates had taken all of the good seats in the middle and the back rows.

"Why don't you sit right here, Drew?" said Brian. He pointed to a seat in the front row near the door.

"Thank you," said Drew. *Great, now everybody can keep staring at me*, he thought. Drew sat up straighter than usual.

Brian closed the classroom door and began the class. "Welcome back, everyone," he said. "Our focus tonight is Rule Seven, passing. The Commissioner informed me that we have a new classmate tonight, Drew Hennings." Brian paused, and everyone greeted Drew. "Drew is thinking about becoming the first teen ref in our board's history."

The responses of the other candidates were polite and encouraging, but they made Drew feel even more uncomfortable. *Maybe the Jamboree will be my last game,* he thought.

Next, Brian handed Drew a rulebook and began talking to the class about the key points of Rule Seven.

Before Drew followed his teacher's instructions, he inspected the book. *Refs have to learn all of this? It's huge!* thought Drew. Brian used a computer slide show to summarize his remarks, and he handed each candidate a printout of the slide show. Occasionally, Brian would stop to take questions or ask the candidates to complete a practice problem. Drew read, "First down and ten yards to go at the offense's own thirty-five yard line. Tight end #88 goes out for a pass. He runs ten yards, and he stops and begins to run back towards the quarterback. While the ball is in the air, linebacker #48 wraps one arm around the tight end and then bats the ball down.

A) There is no foul for defensive pass interference (DPI)

B) Foul for DPI. The penalty is fifteen yards from the previous spot. First down and ten yards to go from the fifty.

C) Foul for DPI. Because the penalty occurred within 15 yards of the line of scrimmage, penalize the defense at the spot of the foul. First down and ten yards to go.

D) Foul for DPI. The penalty is ten yards from the previous spot. First down and ten yards to go from the offense's forty-yard line.

Drew could easily picture the word problem in his head because he had seen this play many times in games that he had played in and in games that he had watched on TV. *Of course it's pass interference. You can't touch the receiver on purpose before he has a chance to catch the ball. Pass interference is a fifteen-yard penalty. The answer is B,* thought Drew.

The correct answer was C. Brian said, "Remember: if defensive pass interference happens within fifteen yards of the line of scrimmage, then penalize it at the spot where the foul occurred."

Drew frowned. *I forgot that part,* he thought. When it came to football, Drew was not used to making mistakes. His competitive juices started to flow, and Drew felt a little surge of energy pulse through his body. He was focused and determined to get the next question right.

Brian's lecture continued, and he stopped when he wanted the candidates to answer another question: "On first down at his own thirty-five-yard line, wide receiver #18 runs deep down the field and cuts for the goal post. Deep into his pass route and while the ball is in the air, #18 starts to outrun the cornerback, #3. The cornerback tackles #18, and the ball falls incomplete nearby.

A) Foul for defensive pass interference (DPI). The penalty is five yards from the previous spot. Second down and five yards to go at the 40-yard line.

B) Foul for DPI. Because the penalty occurred more than fifteen yards away from the line of scrimmage, the foul is fifteen yards from the previous spot. First down and ten yards to go at the fifty-yard line.

C) Foul for DPI. Penalize the defense at the spot of the foul. First down and ten yards to go.

D) There is no foul for defensive pass interference (DPI).

This happened to me and Troy last season, thought Drew. *It's DPI, and it happened more than fifteen yards downfield. The penalty is fifteen yards. First and ten at the fifty,* he thought.

When the officials finished their answers, Brian said, "The answer is B. Our rules are NCAA rules. This is not the National Football League!"

Drew pumped his right fist and said, "Yes!" under his breath. Brian noticed him and smiled.

Did anyone else see that? Drew wondered.

When Brian's lecture was over, the candidates watched game film of case plays that were selected and narrated by the Commissioner from the Southeastern Conference.

This is so much easier to understand than the word problems, Drew thought. Drew enjoyed watching the game film, and he thought, *I would be watching college football on Thursday night anyway. Why not watch football here, and try to make a little money doing it?*

The class ended at 8:30 pm. Drew thanked his teacher and walked out. Jack was waiting for him, and he was standing beside a tall man with silver hair who was wearing khakis and a black polo shirt with the football officials' logo on the left breast.

"Hi, Drew. I'm Commissioner MacLean," he said and stuck out his hand.

Drew shook it. "It's nice to meet you."

"How did class go tonight?" asked the Commissioner.

"Good," Drew said. "The word problems were tough, but I'm getting the hang of it."

"I understand. There's no substitute for game experience," said the Commissioner.

"Drew, the Commissioner wanted to meet you, but he also wanted to talk to you about Sunday's Jamboree in Norwell," said Jack.

"Yes, we'd like you to go. We encourage all of the candidates to attend because it's a clinic for new officials. We will pair you with a more experienced official—" said the Commissioner.

"I will be working with you," added Jack. "I had to argue with John about it."

"The way it will go is that you will stand behind Jack on the sideline and follow him down the field for some of the game, and then you'll switch. You will officiate, and Jack will stand close by to coach you."

"Cool," said Drew.

"So this is something that you're interested in?" asked the Commissioner.

"Yes," Drew said.

"Good," said the Commissioner. "We'll see how it goes, and then we'll take it from there, ok?"

"Sounds good," said Drew.

"Jack, does he have gear?" the Commissioner asked.

"Yes. He needs little things like bean bags and a down counter, but that won't be a problem," Jack said.

"And if this is something that you think you want to pursue more seriously, you can buy a set of cold weather gear," said the Commissioner. "Anyway, the Youth Football Jamboree will give you some great game experience, and there is usually a pretty good crowd there. It'll be fun."

As soon as Drew heard the Commissioner say *crowd*, he felt his stomach do a flip. *What if my friends see me?* he thought. Drew remembered himself and said, "Yeah, it'll be fun. Thanks."

"It's been a long day," said Jack. "It's time to take this young man home so that he can get some rest."

"It was nice to meet you, Drew," said the Commissioner.

"It was nice to meet you too," said Drew. Drew and Jack walked down the stairs and outside to the parking lot.

Chapter 9
PRACTICING COURAGE

As Jack and Drew drove home, Jack said, "Drew, you didn't sound very enthusiastic about working the Jamboree. Are you sure that you want to do this?"

I thought that I hid it well enough, Drew thought. "Really?" he asked.

"Yes," said Jack. "Do you want to talk about it?"

"Thanks, Uncle Jack. I already talked about it a lot with my parents. It's the same stuff. I know that Hingham Youth Football will be at the Jamboree, and I know that some of my friends will be there watching their younger siblings," said Drew.

"You're worried that your friends are going to make fun of you?"

"Yes," said Drew. "I can take it, but, and I mean no offense Uncle Jack, I just don't know if it's worth it. You know?"

"You mean that if you loved officiating football, then it would be easier not to care what other people think, but you don't know if you love it," said Jack.

"Yeah," said Drew.

"Sounds like a lot of pressure to put on yourself," said Jack. "Zora Neal Hurston once said, 'You've got to go there to know there.' Be patient with yourself. You'll find the answer. Did you like skiing the first time that you did it?"

"I hated it," said Drew.

"Do you still hate it?" asked Jack.

"No. I love it," said Drew.

"Why?" asked Jack.

"Because I got good at it."

"I don't want to give away the answer, but my guess is that the same thing will happen with officiating football," said Jack. "Listen, I just thought of one other thing that you need to know before you make your decision: you've got to be brave to do what we do. When you officiate, you have to do what you believe is right even when you know that your decision is going to make a lot of people unhappy. You're never too young to practice courage, and you've got to have courage if you're going to be a leader someday."

Drew nodded, but he did not say anything. Soon the car pulled into Drew's driveway. He thanked Jack and went inside. That night Drew had trouble sleeping. He lay staring at the ceiling with his head on his hands. *It's one thing to say that you don't care what your friends think. It's another thing to act like it. Is reffing worth all of this drama? Are they even still my friends?* He rolled on his side, but he couldn't get comfortable. *Jack's right: I won't know until I go to the Jamboree and see what happens.* He rolled onto his other side. *The waiting is the worst part,* he thought. Although it had been a long, tiring day, Drew didn't fall asleep for a long time.

On Friday Drew sat with his friends at lunch. He was the only one at the table without his freshman football jersey on, and he felt pretty low. The talk was about the first home game that started right after school.

"Are you coming to watch us?" Troy asked.

That's the last place on earth that I want to be, thought Drew. "I can't," he lied. My parents want me to watch Libby until they get home." There was an uncomfortable silence.

"Want to meet up after the game?" asked Scott.

"Sure," said Drew.

When the school day ended, the campus was alive, and the parking lot was still full. The weather was beautiful, and there were games all over the athletic fields: field hockey, boys' soccer, cross country, and the freshman football game. Drew felt left out and ashamed that he wasn't playing. He watched out the window as his bus pulled onto Union Street, and he put in his headphones.

Drew didn't speak to anyone for the entire ride. When he got home, he was alone for the first time all day. Drew sat at the kitchen table and cried. After he was done, he felt better. Without quite knowing why, he went upstairs to his bedroom. He saw the football rulebook on his desk, and he stared at it. Suddenly, Jack's words came back to him, "You're never too young to practice courage."

Drew knew what he had to do. He quickly changed into his workout gear, and left a note on the kitchen counter, "**Went for a run. Be back soon. Love, Drew.**" Drew grabbed his phone and his ear buds and walked out the front door. He turned on the music, and as soon as he reached the end of his driveway, he started to run. He had no route or destination. *You're worthless. You're a loser. You're already forgotten. Everyone is going to laugh at you*, he thought. These thoughts played over and over again in his head. The music couldn't stop them, so he turned it off. Drew ran until he couldn't hear his thoughts anymore. He was soaked with sweat, and he could only hear the sound of his feet pounding the pavement and the rhythm of his own breathing. Drew enjoyed the simple beauty of not feeling like a failure anymore.

He turned around and ran home. As he neared his driveway, he sprinted, and he finished his run with a yell of triumph.

By now his parents and Libby were home. He quickly said hello and ran upstairs to shower. When he finished, he was starving, and he went to the kitchen for a snack.

"How was school today?" his Mom asked.

"Good. Not as hot as it was last week," he said.

"Do you have a lot of homework?" she asked.

"Same as usual," he said.

"Just make sure that you get it done before your game on Sunday, ok?" Mom said.

"Ok," said Drew.

"What time is the game?" she asked.

"Noon," he said.

"It's probably going to last until about four p.m." said his Dad. "You're probably going to be beat when you get home."

"We're going to go to church too. It's the annual Water Service," said Mom.

"Got it," said Drew.

"Are you meeting up with the boys tonight?" asked Dad.

"No," said Drew. "I'm going to stay in. I've got to study the rulebook and get ready for Sunday."

Dad and Mom looked at each other and smiled. Mom said, "Libby has soccer practice at the Ward Street Field, and then she is going over to a friend's house. Your father and I were going to go out for dinner in the Harbor. Are you ok here?"

"Can I order a pizza?" Drew asked.

"Sure," Mom said.

Shortly afterward, Drew was alone in his living room with an empty pizza box and sports drink on the coffee table and his

NCAA Rulebook beside him. He got a text from Troy, "We won 20-7. Brendan ran for 2 TDs. I scored the other. We are going to Scott's house. You coming?"

Drew wrote back, "Can't make it out tonight, but congrats on the win." Drew was watching college football on TV, and every time there was a penalty, Drew would look up the rule in the book and read it. At every commercial break, he would do ten push-ups. When his family came home, they saw him reading the rulebook and left him alone. By the fourth quarter, Drew could barely keep his eyes open. When he was done with his study session, he went up to bed. He opened his windows wide to let the cool night air into his room. Drew set his alarm for 7a.m., and he fell asleep.

It felt to Drew like only moments had passed, and his alarm went off. As difficult as it was, he got out of bed and went downstairs. His Dad was already there.

"What's got you up so early?" he asked.

"Dad, can you drive me to the school at 8:45a.m.? I want to try and ref some flag games to get ready for tomorrow," asked Drew.

"Sure," said Dad. "How did the studying go last night?"

"It went ok. I tried to watch the game like I was reffing it. When there was a penalty, I would look it up in the rulebook and read about it," said Drew.

"That's a good idea, but I'm a bit surprised. I thought that you didn't like reffing that much," said Dad.

"Maybe it's like everything else: it's more fun when you get good at it. Besides, it beats sitting around feeling sorry for myself," Drew said.

"Yeah, I know that the freshman team had its first game last night. That must have been hard for you," said Dad.

Drew tried to answer, but his eyes filled with tears, and all he could do was nod his head.

Dad put his hand on his shoulder, "Keep fighting, kid. I'm proud of you."

Drew nodded again. Dad rose from the table and kissed Drew on the top of his head.

Shortly after breakfast Dad drove Drew to the high school.

"Can you wait here for a minute?" asked Drew.

"Sure thing," said Dad.

Just like the week before, eight officials were standing in a circle near midfield. Drew approached and was relieved to see John. Drew jogged over to the group, and John was in the middle of a story. When he saw Drew he said, "Fellas, here's the teen ref I was telling you about."

"Hey guys," said Drew. "John, do you mind if I work some games with you guys for community service? I could really use the practice before tomorrow's Jamboree."

"Fellas, I'm putting him on my crew. We'll work with three men," said John. He continued telling his story about an extra point that got blown back through the uprights on a windy night at Hull High School. "The crossbar is a line, not a plane. The kick has to cross the line and stay there. The extra point was no good!" he said.

There's a rule about that? That would never happen. John's making that up, Drew thought. Drew jogged back to his Dad, updated him, and asked for a ride home at noon. Drew spent the next two hours working with John. It was just like the week before. Drew worked on using the whistle correctly, spotting the ball, "squaring into" the center of the field, staying in the proper position, and using the proper hand signals to count the downs. Just like the week before, the kids loved him. John even taught Drew how to "kill the clock." He told Drew, "When the ball goes out of bounds, wave your hands over your head, and criss-cross them a couple of times. This signals the rest of the crew and the clock operator that the ball is out of bounds and that the clock should stop." Drew did as he was told, and soon he was "killing the clock" like any experienced referee.

Towards the end of the second game, one of the second graders caught a short pass close to the sideline. As the receiver turned to run downfield, the defender took his flag and ended the play. Drew trailed the play, "squared in" towards the spot of the ball, and blew his whistle. He looked across the field at John, and John signaled for a timeout. Next, John motioned for Drew to jog over and conference with him. *What's going on? It was a routine play*, thought Drew.

John saw the confusion in his face, and said, "Relax. You didn't do anything wrong. I want to teach you another signal."

"Oh," said Drew.

"Plays often end close to the sideline, just like that one. You may know that the ball is still inbounds, but the officials on your crew can't see it. What you should do is blow the whistle, and give a 'wind the clock' motion. Just move your arm backwards in a big circle," said Jack.

"When I played quarterback, I used to do something like that to warm up my throwing arm," said Drew.

"If that helps you remember the signal, then that's great," said John. "I remember it because the lead guitarist of The Who used to do it when he had a big solo."

"Who?" Drew asked.

"No, The Who. It's a famous band," said John. "You kids don't know your Classic Rock. Get back to your sideline, Hennings."

"Yes, sir," said Drew.

The game continued, and once again, Drew put his new lesson into action without making a mistake. At the end of the game, the players thanked Drew, and he slapped fives and bumped knuckles with them.

John said, "You officiate like that at the Jamboree, and you're going to be alright."

"Thanks," said Drew.

"Thanks for the help. I'd keep you here for the third game, but I'm worried that the other officials will get mad at me," said John.

Drew smiled, and he jogged to the adjacent field.

"Good luck tomorrow, Drew!" said John.

"Thanks!" said Drew over his shoulder.

Drew ran to the other field, introduced himself to the new crew, and got to work. Drew was tired, but he stayed focused and worked hard. He gave the kids another good game, and once again they showed their appreciation. After the game, Drew saw his dad pull up to the entrance of the stadium.

"That's my ride. Thanks, guys," he said. Drew turned and jogged for the parking lot. Behind him Drew heard one of the officials call out, "Good game, kid!"

As Drew walked out of the stadium, he thought, *That felt good. Not as good as playing football with my friends and scoring touchdowns, but it felt good. Anyway, it beats sitting around feeling sorry for myself.* When Drew reached the car, his Dad asked, "How'd it go?"

"We'll see tomorrow," said Drew.

"Let's get you home so that you can get some rest," Dad said, and they drove off.

However, Drew did not rest when he got home. He showered and ate lunch, and then he did his homework. Dad and Mom saw him working at the kitchen table and looked at each other dumbfounded. Drew finished his homework at three o'clock, just before the kickoff of the Michigan vs. Cincinnati game. He had an ice cold Arnold Palmer on the coffee table and his rulebook on the couch beside him. Just as the Wolverine offense was taking the field for its first drive, Drew got a text from Scott. "Hanging out at my pool. You in?"

Drew stared at his phone for a while. Mom walked back into the living room. She saw Drew, and she said, "Are you all right?"

Drew leaned back and ran his hands through his hair and looked at the ceiling, "No. I don't know."

Mom sat down on the couch. She waited. Drew didn't say anything. After a while she said, "Dad told me that the team had its first game without you and that you took it pretty hard."

"Yeah," said Drew.

"You loved that team," Mom said.

"Yeah," said Drew. He felt tears well up in his eyes.

Mom waited. "It seems like it's more complicated than that," she said.

"Yeah," said Drew. "I wish that I could play again. They're so lucky," said Drew.

"They can still play, and you can't, and that makes you feel jealous?" Mom asked.

"Yeah," said Drew. It was getting easier for him to talk about it now. "Troy texted me last night, and he told me that they won 20-7. We used to score twenty points in the first half!"

"I remember," said Mom. "They could use your help, but you can't help them. It's frustrating."

"It just makes me so mad. Why did this happen? It's not fair!" shouted Drew.

"No, it isn't. You're allowed to be mad." She patted his hand. It was silent for a while, and Mom said, "Was there something in that text that upset you?"

"It didn't upset me," said Drew. "Last night Troy invited me over, and I said 'no,' and now Scott just invited me to his pool. I know, it's stupid—"

"It's not stupid," said Mom.

"It's just stresses me out. It sounds ridiculous. It's like 'get a real problem, Drew,' but it just feels like more drama, and I don't want any more drama right now," he said.

"So you don't want to hang out with them this weekend?" said Mom.

"Right," said Drew.

"Then don't," said Mom.

"But I'm not on the team anymore, and I don't hang out with them as much as I used to. If I keep saying 'no' every time that they want to hang out, then they'll stop asking me, and I won't have any friends," said Drew.

"Whoa. Take it easy. You guys have been friends for a long time. It sounds like this weekend you just need some space to figure things out," said Mom.

"Yeah," he said.

"Then take it. It's ok to focus on you every once in a while. Don't worry about your friends. They will still be there on Monday," said Mom.

"I guess."

"Besides, now that I know how you're feeling, I wouldn't let you go over there anyway. You can blame me if you want to. I mean, can you imagine? Scott would ask you if you wanted some chips, and you would just explode. There'd be fights and blood everywhere. The sharks would start circling in the water. You don't want that at a pool party. It's not a good time," Mom said.

Drew laughed. "I don't think that there are sharks in Scott's pool," he said.

"Are you sure? I thought that you told me he had a pet shark," she said.

"No," said Drew.

"It must have been one of your other friends," she said. "Or maybe it was somewhere that we went on vacation. Who can remember it all?"

Drew laughed again. Mom gave him a hug. "I know that this is a hard time for you, but you're doing great. I love you," she said.

"Love you too, Mom," Drew said. It felt like a weight had been lifted off of Drew's chest. When she had gone, Drew texted Scott, "Worked all morning. Too tired. Thanks for the invite." He put his phone down and turned on the TV to watch the football game. While he watched, he repeated what he had done the night before. When there was a penalty, Drew found the penalty in the rulebook and read about it. At halftime Drew fell asleep. When he woke up, the game was almost over. Drew was a little annoyed that he had slept for so long, but he felt great.

He planned to watch the rest of the fourth quarter, but Drew noticed a note on the coffee table, "We went to the Murray's for a barbecue. Join us when you wake up. Love, Mom"

Drew checked the time, and it was almost 6 p.m. He turned off the TV and raced upstairs to change and get ready. Minutes later he was out the door and jogging up the street to his neighbor's house. Drew jogged through the Murray's side yard and joined everyone on the back deck.

"Hi. Sorry I'm late," he said.

"Dad was just going to go back to the house and check on you," said Mom.

Claire Murray, Drew's classmate, was sitting on the opposite side of the deck. She wore her blond hair down, and she used her sunglasses like a headband. She looked pretty and bored.

Drew walked over and said, "Hey, Claire."

"You left me alone with parents and middle schoolers," she said. She did not look up from her phone.

"Sorry about that. Where are Maddie and Libby?"

"Inside," said Claire.

"How was your field hockey game yesterday? What position do you play again?" Drew asked.

"Defense," she said. "The other team scored a goal, but we played well enough to win," Claire said.

"Do you have any more games this weekend?" Drew asked.

"No. We have the weekend off," she said.

"So what have you been up to?" asked Drew.

"I volunteered at the animal shelter this morning then I came home and did my homework," Claire said.

Drew rolled his eyes. "Claire's day off," he said.

"Like you should judge. I heard your parents say that you did your homework this afternoon, too!" she said.

"I have a confession to make: I actually did homework on a Saturday," said Drew. "Then I passed out. My body was so confused that it just shut down," he said.

Claire laughed. "I don't get it. Are you going to the Patriots' game tomorrow or something?"

"No. If I were going to Foxboro, I'd just do my homework on the car ride."

"Or on the bus ride to school on Monday morning," she said. "Or not at all."

"Exactly," said Drew.

"So what's up?" she asked.

"Community service," said Drew. "Tomorrow afternoon."

"I can't believe this: Drew Hennings getting an early start on an assignment. Did you hit your head again or something?" said Claire.

"No," said Drew. He stopped smiling.

Claire looked Drew in the eyes and quickly looked away. After a pause, Claire said, "So are you going to tell me what you're doing, or is it some big secret?"

Drew took a deep breath and looked down, "I'm going to referee youth football."

"That's cute. When I was in fourth grade, the high school field hockey players used to ref our scrimmages. We thought they were goddesses."

Clueless as usual. She means well, though, thought Drew.

"I bet all of the little cheerleaders are going to fall madly in love with you. Who is that handsome boy in the striped shirt?

106

Maybe they'll ask you for your autograph at the end of the game," said Claire.

Drew laughed. It felt good to tell someone his own age what he was up to. *That didn't go so badly,* he thought. He said, "I was thinking I would bring a permanent marker so that I could sign some pom-poms after the game. Maybe I could autograph one of my penalty flags and throw it to the crowd when I'm done?"

"It's brilliant. Go with it," she said.

Drew thought about the crowd at the Jamboree. *When my friends see me tomorrow, it's just not going to go well,* he thought. Drew started to feel nervous again.

"Drew, are you all right?" asked Claire.

"Yeah, sorry. I just zoned out for a second," he said. Claire giggled and changed the topic. Claire and Drew ate and talked. Drew listened eagerly for any news about Callie. However, Claire talked about her field hockey team, and Callie was on the Dance Team. The night swam by, and when it was time to go home, Drew thought, *I haven't thought about football in a while. Cool.*

Chapter 10

SEASON OPENER

On Saturday night Drew had trouble sleeping again. He had a nightmare. He was reffing a game, and he heard laughter coming from the stands. Drew tried to ignore it, but it followed him down the field, and it kept getting louder. Soon the noise was right behind him, and Drew turned around. All of his friends were there: Troy, Scott, Brendan, and Claire. The entire eighth grade football team was there, and Callie was there with all of the cheerleaders.

Scott spoke first, "He was the star quarterback, and look at him now."

"What a loser," said Callie. They continued to point and laugh. Someone threw something at Drew. He couldn't tell what it was, but he was able to dodge it. Drew turned around and tried to focus on the game. He thought that he had only turned around for a moment, but he had missed several plays. Jack was in the middle of the field looking annoyed. A running back ran to Drew's side and got tackled by his facemask. Drew froze. He didn't throw the flag.

He heard Claire's voice behind him, "Are you sure that you can help these kids? Do you even know the rules?"

Drew turned back to the field, and he was greeted by an angry coach. "How could you miss that call? What are you stupid?"

Drew lost his temper and charged the coach. The next thing that he knew they were on the ground. Jack had to pull Drew off of the coach. Next, the police ran onto the field and handcuffed

Drew. All of Drew's friends watched as he was escorted off of the field.

Scott repeated, "He used to be a star. Look at him now."

Drew's parents woke him up. It was 9 a.m. on Sunday morning, and he had to get ready to go to the Old Ship Church. *I didn't get in a fight. I didn't get arrested. I didn't humiliate myself in front of all of my friends.* Drew had never felt so good about waking up early on a Sunday morning. When Drew walked inside the church, his eyes adjusted to the darkness of the nearly four hundred-year-old, wooden meeting house. The boards creaked under his feet. The familiar sights and sounds were peaceful, but as Drew slowly woke up, he felt a knot in his stomach. The minister took the pulpit to deliver a sermon about hope, however, Drew's one hope was that the Reverend would hurry up.

After service, Drew got home and changed for the game. Shortly afterwards, Jack was in his driveway, and Dad came out to talk to them.

"I'll have him back around 4 p.m.," said Jack.

"Thanks, Jack," said Dad.

"Dad, no surprise visits this time, o.k.?" said Drew.

"I promise," he said. "But I get a full report after tonight's Patriots' game, right?"

"Sure," said Drew.

"Jack, the game is at 4:30p.m., and we're eating chili in front of the TV. Do you want to join us?" asked Dad.

"Thanks for the invite, Mike," said Jack. "But I promised Mary that we would go out to dinner in the Shipyard."

"Just thought I'd ask," said Dad. "Good luck, guys."

Drew and Jack drove to Norwell High School for the Youth Football Jamboree. When they arrived, it was difficult to find a parking space. It was a long walk from the parking lot to the football field, and Drew pulled the brim of his hat down and walked quickly. He and Jack reached the gate, walked onto the field, and joined the twenty officials who were already gathered there. The Commissioner stood in the middle of the group and gave instructions. The Jamboree would begin with the youngest age group, grades three and four. Two scrimmages would run simultaneously on opposite ends of the field so that four teams could play at the same time. Four teams would play for the first quarter, and four new teams would play for the second quarter. At half time the teams would switch opponents. During the second half, each team would play for one more period. The seventh and eighth grade games would follow, and the fifth and sixth grade games would end the Jamboree. After the Commissioner explained the format, he paired new officials with mentors and sent half of the officials to one end of the field and the other half to the opposite end.

Jack and Drew jogged towards the Hanover and Abington teams. The Hanover Warriors wore blue and gold, and the Abington Green Wave wore green and white. Jack took the field first, and Drew stood three yards behind him on the sideline. Jack talked over his shoulder, "Our position on the crew is called the Line Judge. We count the defense and watch the line of scrimmage."

The scrimmage began. After the first play, Jack said, "Count the defensive players after every down to make sure that they have eleven. When you're finished, stick out the arm closest to the defense and give a thumbs up. It tells your crewmates that the defense has the correct number of players. The official on the other side of the field, he's called the Head Linesman, will see your signal, and if he has also counted eleven players, then he will tip his cap. Then you know that your team is ready to play."

"Got it," said Drew. He could hear the crowd getting louder and louder behind him. *Don't look back*, he thought. After a few more plays, Drew asked, "Hey, Jack,"

"Yeah," Jack said over his shoulder.

"What if the team I'm counting doesn't have eleven players?"

"You tell me: can you play with ten players?" asked Jack.

"Yes," said Drew.

"Can you play with twelve?" asked Jack.

"No," said Drew.

"What's the penalty?" asked Jack.

"Five yards," said Drew.

"Yes, but what's it called?" asked Jack.

"Too many men on the field?" said Drew.

"Substitution Infraction," said Jack. "Try to blow the whistle and prevent the play from starting. You don't want anyone to get hurt."

"Got it," said Drew.

"Do you know what the signal for it is?" asked Jack.

"No idea," said Drew.

"Put your hand on your heart like you're saluting the flag."

Drew was silent. *That's a lot to remember*, he thought.

"Do you want to take over?" asked Jack.

"Already?" Drew asked. He took Jack's place, and his heart started pounding. *Count the players on defense*, he thought. He had barely finished when the play started. The same thing happened on the next play.

"Drew, count them in groups. It moves faster. I usually count three, three, three, two," said Jack.

Drew did as he was told, and it gave him enough time to signal the Head Linesman as well. On the next play the Hanover offense ran a toss sweep to Drew's side. Drew trailed the play, and Drew "killed the clock" when the player went out of bounds.

"Nice work, Drew. Who taught you that?"

"I worked with John yesterday at flag football," said Drew. Drew's nerves were beginning to calm down. The next play was a run up the middle that gained six yards. Drew "squared in," and Jack complimented him again. The Hanover running back ran another sweep towards Drew and broke free for a twenty-yard touchdown run. Drew watched the play, put on a burst of speed and raced the runner to the end zone. He signaled touchdown, and the crowd cheered loudly.

Jack approached Drew and said, "You've got great speed, but you can't see the whole play when you're in a footrace with the running back."

"Sorry," said Drew. "I just wanted to get the nerves out." He smiled.

The Abington offense took over, and they also scored a touchdown. Drew was in proper position this time. The quarter ended, and two new teams took the field. The Norwell Clippers were playing the Rockland Bulldogs. Norwell wore blue and gold, and Rockland wore blue and white. Jack officiated a few plays and then let Drew take over. Drew's counting of players, counting of the downs, use of the whistle, and positioning were all solid. At half time the Commissioner approached Jack and Drew, and he said, "You look sharp, Drew. Jack, you weren't kidding. This kid can run!"

"Thank you," said Drew. Only now, during a break in the action, did Drew think about the crowd. He turned briefly to look at the stands, and he saw a lot of Hingham red. *They don't know you're here. Just keep your back turned, don't make any stupid mistakes, and you'll be fine*, he thought.

In the third quarter Hanover and Rockland came onto the field. Drew impressed Jack by using the "wind the clock" signal when an Abington runner got tackled inbounds near the sidelines.

"Did John teach you that too?" asked Jack.

"Yup," said Drew with a smile.

"He made my job easy!" said Jack.

The remainder of the scrimmage passed without incident. As Drew was drinking water and waiting for the seventh and eighth grade game to start, Jack tried to prepare him, "You played against some of these guys last year. This is going to be the toughest job of the day."

"Understood," said Drew. He felt anxious but confident.

In the seventh and eighth grade game the Barnstable Red Raiders from Cape Cod played against the Middleboro Sachems. The Hingham Harbormen and the Hanson Warriors played on the other half of the field. Jack and Drew worked with Barnstable and Middleboro. Barnstable wore red and white, and Middleboro wore black and orange. *The Hingham fans won't look over here. Thank you, football gods!* thought Drew. The game began, and Drew's stomach turned. *This is so much faster than the other game!* he thought. Jack officiated the first five minutes of the quarter and switched places with Drew. On the first play, Drew hadn't finished counting eleven players on defense, and Barnstable snapped the ball. On the next play, Drew finished counting the players, but he forgot to "square in" when he spotted the ball.

On the third play, the runner was tackled right in front of Drew, and Drew forgot to blow his whistle.

Jack pulled Drew aside. Drew felt his cheeks and ears turning red. *Everyone's looking at me!* he thought. Drew said, "It's too fast. I can't keep up."

"Yes, you can," said Jack. "You just need to settle down. When you played quarterback, do you remember how you used to prepare for each play?"

"Yeah, I would check to make sure that my offense was in the right position, then I would check the defense. I would figure out if they were playing man or zone, and I would begin the cadence."

"Exactly. You always did the same thing: you calmed yourself and focused on what you had to do. Officiating is no different," said Jack.

Barnstable ran another play, and Drew looked alarmed. "There are eight other officials watching the game. It's fine," said Jack. He continued, "I prepare for every play the same way. I answer these questions: where is the ball? What down is it? How many yards does the offense need to make a first down? Does my team have eleven players?" said Jack.

"Field position, down, distance, player count. Got it," said Drew.

"Try it before every play. It will help you," said Jack.

Drew did as he was told, and after a few plays he was officiating as well as he had in the first game. He looked back at Jack and smiled, and Jack nodded. The quarter ended, and the teams switched. In the second quarter the Hull Pirates played the West Bridgewater Wildcats. Hull wore blue and gold, and West

Bridgewater wore maroon and white. Jack officiated for a few plays and turned the duties over to Drew.

Drew took his place and began his pre-snap routine. *It's first down and ten yards to go. The ball is on the twenty-seven-yard line, and West Bridgewater needs to get to the seventeen to get a first down. Three-three-three-two. Hull has eleven players on defense,* thought Drew. He took a deep breath and watched the play. The Wildcats ran a power play behind the right tackle. Their fullback ran through the line, hit the Hull linebacker, and turned him sideways. The running back ran right behind his lead blocker, and cut to the outside, directly in front of Drew. Just then the Hull defensive back jumped on the runner and dragged him down. As the runner fell, Drew could see the defender's hand on the runner's facemask. *Did the defender grab the running back's facemask?* Drew froze.

Close by he heard the West Bridgewater coach yell, "That's a facemask! That's a facemask! Come on, ref!"

Next, Drew saw a yellow penalty flag fly past him onto the field. Jack had thrown it. He approached Drew and said, "You've got to throw that flag, Drew. We've got to keep the players safe."

"I wasn't sure—" said Drew.

"Don't be afraid to make a mistake, especially when you're trying to keep the players safe," said Jack. "Now, tell me what happened."

"There was a Facemask penalty on the defense," said Drew.

"Did you get the number of the player who grabbed the facemask?" asked Jack.

"Ah…no," said Drew. "It was the defensive back."

"Ok, say that to the referee. Where did the penalty happen?" Jack asked.

Drew looked down. "It happened right here at the twenty-yard line."

"Good. You're going to have to tell that to the referee too," said Jack.

"What's the result of the penalty?" asked Jack.

"It's a fifteen-yard penalty," said Drew.

"It is," said Jack. "But think about where we are on the field."

Drew thought out loud, "The penalty will leave the ball at the five-yard line."

Jack waited for Drew to find the correct answer.

"That's too close!" said Drew. "The penalty can't bring the ball closer than half the distance to the goal line."

"Good," said Jack. "Now go and tell the referee what happened."

Drew jogged over to the referee. They talked for a while, and Drew returned.

"How did it go?" asked Jack.

"I think that I talked too much," said Drew. "He just wanted me to tell him who, what, and where." Jack and Drew walked to the ten-yard line to set up for the next play. "This is a lot to think about," said Drew.

"Yes, it is. That's why you have to stay calm and focused," said Jack. "Now get ready for the next play. Go through your pre-snap routine."

Drew did as he was told, and he did not have time to dwell on the fact that he had actually missed throwing his penalty flag on the last play.

Drew worked the rest of the second quarter and the remainder of the game without making any significant mistakes. When the third and final game of the day began, the fifth and sixth grade game, Drew was hungry and tired. However, if the first game had been too slow, and the second game had been too fast, then the third game was just right. Drew effectively used his pre-snap routine and all of the lessons that he had learned over the last week. For the first time all day, he felt completely confident and focused. Jack let Drew officiate the entire second half. In the fourth quarter the East Bridgewater Vikings took the field to play the Pembroke Titans. East Bridgewater wore baby blue and gold, and Pembroke wore blue and red. Pembroke struck first. They drove steadily down the field and punched the ball in after two runs from the three-yard line. East Bridgewater answered with a sustained drive of its own, and with under two minutes left, the Vikings had the ball first down and goal to go from the eight-yard line. Two runs off tackle advanced the ball to the four-yard line.

With each play the crowd grew louder. On third down the Vikings ran a sweep to the left side of the field, away from Drew. The runner got tackled by his ankles before he reached the original line of scrimmage. It was fourth and goal from the six-yard line, and East Bridgewater called timeout. When the timeout ended, the Vikings quickly huddled and jogged to the line of scrimmage.

Drew tried to block out the noise behind him with his pre-snap routine: *it's fourth and goal from the six. Three-three-three-two makes eleven. The defense has eleven men on the field,* he thought. He took a deep breath. *If it were my team, then I would throw the ball,* he thought. The center snapped the football, and the quarterback sprinted to his right. Drew took a big step towards the end zone, and out of the corner of his eye he saw the East Bridgewater receiver sprint, gather his feet underneath him, and make a sharp cut to the sideline. Drew jogged to the goal line pylon and stopped. He kept one eye on the quarterback and the other on the receiver. Drew saw the quarterback pull up and fire a pass to the end zone. Drew immediately shifted his view to the receiver and saw that the defender had caught up with his man. With his left arm the defender grabbed the back of the receiver's shirt. He used his leverage to turn the receiver's body just enough so that the defender could reach around the receiver's torso and bat the ball down.

The defender grabbed him from behind while the ball was in the air! thought Drew, and he threw his penalty flag at the feet of the two players. Drew blew his whistle three times to signal to the other official that there had been a penalty, and he jogged to the referee to report what he had seen, "Pass interference on the defense," he said.

"Where did it happen?" asked the referee.

"There," said Drew, and he pointed to where the yellow flag lay on the ground.

"In the end zone," asked the referee.

"Yes," said Drew.

"Do you know what that means?"

Drew looked confused.

The referee explained, "When the ball is inside the seventeen-yard line, and pass interference happens at or inside of the two yard line, then we place the ball at the two yard line for the next play."

"Weird. Shouldn't it just be half the distance to the goal like every other penalty?" asked Drew.

"That would make sense wouldn't it? People sometimes think that we're fools, but some of these rules are so complicated, and there are so many of them, that it's hard to remember it all," said the referee.

Just then Drew noticed the Pembroke coach yelling from the sidelines, "How could he interfere? He batted the ball down. Come on, Ref!"

"Don't worry. I'll talk to him. Good work, kid," said the referee.

"Thanks," said Drew.

When Drew returned to his sideline, Jack said, "Don't forget to keep officiating after a penalty happens. You forgot to signal that the pass was incomplete."

"Oops," said Drew.

"It takes practice," said Jack.

East Bridgewater got the ball on the two-yard line, and they scored on a run up the middle. The scrimmage ended in a 6-6 tie.

Chapter 11
POSTGAME CONFERENCES

Jack and Drew walked to the middle of the field where Commissioner MacLean addressed the candidates and their mentors. When he finished speaking, all of the officials walked off of the field together. When Jack and Drew reached the gate, the Commissioner said, "I just wanted to check in and see how things went."

"It was good. I had fun," said Drew.

"You made a good call on the pass interference penalty in the end zone," said the Commissioner.

"Thanks," said Drew.

"You have great speed too," said the Commissioner. "How do you think he did, Jack?"

"I thought that he did well. He struggled a little with the pace of the seventh and eighth grade game, but once I taught him about pre-snap routines, he settled down," said Jack.

"I saw that," said Commissioner MacLean. "Drew, we've never had an official as young as you in the E.M.A.F.O. You've got great physical talent, a love for the game, and you're smart. That said, in the seventh and eighth grade games you're working with players who are only a year or two younger than you are. That's tough. Moving forward, and Jack I'm wondering what you think of this, if Drew chooses to keep officiating, then maybe we should focus his work on flag games, and youth games for grades two through six."

"I agree with you. Drew should not officiate the seventh and eighth games until he has more experience, and he's a little older. Maybe he could be the clock operator for those games?"

"That could work. Drew could also work on the Chain Crew. I could leave that to you and Drew to decide. You'll still mentor him, right Jack?"

"Of course," Jack said.

"The most important thing to consider is this," the Commissioner continued, "Do you want to keep officiating football?"

Drew's eyes grew wide. He did not know what to say.

Jack jumped in, "It's a lot to think about, and he should talk to his parents first. When do you need an answer, Commish?"

"I know that it's not a lot of time, but I assign officials to the youth games on Monday nights. Drew, can you call me tomorrow night and let me know your answer?"

"Yes," said Drew.

"Great," the Commissioner said. "You had a good idea, Jack. E.M.A.F.O is struggling to recruit young officials, and Drew's got talent."

"Thanks for giving him a tryout," said Jack. "It's a new idea in football, but soccer has used teen refs for a long time. They work with elementary school players."

"Maybe football is missing an opportunity. Maybe we'll start a trend. Who knows? It may become a great chance for teens to serve their communities and learn some leadership skills too," said the Commissioner.

"We're visionaries," said Jack.

"What we are," said the Commissioner, "is almost late for the kickoff of the Patriots' game. Good job today, Drew. Talk things over with your folks, and give me a call tomorrow night, ok? Jack, you'll give him my number?"

"Yes, sir. Thanks again," said Jack.

"Thank you," said Drew.

The Commissioner said goodbye and walked towards the parking lot. Jack and Drew were following him until Drew heard, "What are you doing in that outfit?" Drew arched his back like someone had just poured ice water down his shirt.

Drew turned around and saw Scott standing there wearing a Hingham Football t-shirt.

"I'll go get us some drinks at the concessions stand," said Jack, and he left.

After he had gone, Drew said, "Learning how to officiate. What are you doing in that outfit?"

The question caught Scott off guard and gave Drew a chance to recover from the surprise. "I'm here watching my younger brother," Scott said. "I can't believe it. You're a ref," he said.

"It's community service, and sometimes I get paid," said Drew.

"Yeah, but you're a *ref*," said Scott.

"You already said that," said Drew. He wasn't embarrassed, he was annoyed. "Think of it this way, Scott: you had to pay to get in here, and you watched the game from the stands. I got in for free, and I got to watch the game from the field."

"It's just *weird*," said Scott.

"Did you know that the refs earn fifty bucks a game?" Drew asked.

Scott looked surprised. "That's not bad," he said.

"I need community service hours and money. I know a few things about football. You put it all together, and here I am," said Drew.

Scott was silent. Then Scott said, "Is this why you wouldn't hang out with us this weekend? Were you studying the rules or something?"

Drew didn't say anything, and he felt his cheeks turn red.

"I should be mad at you for ditching us this weekend, but it's just too weird," said Scott. He turned, began to walk away, and said to himself, "Drew's a teen ref."

"I was at a neighborhood barbecue on Saturday night!" Drew said to his back. He took a deep breath. *The worst is over,* he thought.

Then Drew heard a girl's voice say, "What are you doing here?"

Drew turned around, and he saw Callie Walker. Drew's stomach dropped like he was on the Tower of Terror at Disney's Hollywood Studios. Callie was wearing red and white, and her dark hair was tied back in a ponytail. Without thinking Drew took off his referee hat and hid it behind his back.

"Well—ahhhh—community service. I ref the little kids' games for community service," said Drew.

"I've never seen a kid our age ref football before," she said.

"My dad knows a guy," said Drew. He quickly changed the subject, "What are you doing here?"

"Same thing, actually," she said.

"You're reffing too?" he said.

She laughed. "No. For community service I help coach the fifth and sixth grade cheerleaders," said Callie.

"Cool," said Drew.

"Yeah. Well, I'll see you at school tomorrow?" she said.

"Yeah. See you at school, Drew said.

"Ok. Bye," Callie said, and she waved.

"Bye," said Drew. He held up his right hand, but he was still holding his referee hat. He quickly switched the hat to his left hand and thrust it behind his back. "Bye," Drew said, and he waved. The thrill of talking to Callie was quickly replaced by self doubt: *She likes athletes, not volunteer referees. You don't have a chance,* he thought.

Moments later Jack returned and handed Drew a sports drink. "You ok?" he asked.

"Yeah," said Drew.

"Let's get you home before the Patriots' game starts," said Jack, and they walked up the long dirt pathway towards the parking lot.

When Drew got home, he rushed upstairs to shower and change. Dad came out to talk to Jack, and Jack filled him in on the Commissioner's idea. Jack also gave Drew's Dad the Commissioner's phone number. That night, after the Patriots' game, Dad and Mom sent Libby upstairs to finish her homework, and they talked with Drew about his first game as a football official.

"Jack told me about the Commissioner's plan, and I filled Mom in. So what do you think? Do you want to go ahead with it?" Dad asked.

Drew was still looking at the muted television. It was replaying highlights from the day's games. Drew said, "I don't know."

"What's holding you back, Drew? Jack told me about all of the compliments that you've been getting: he's big; he's strong;

he's fast; he knows the game; he gets along great with the kids. It seems like a good fit to me," said Dad.

"Are you embarrassed?" asked Mom.

"It's not exactly the coolest thing in the world to do," Drew said. Drew looked at the floor.

"But you will make it cool," said Mom.

"I'm not so sure about that," said Drew.

"What makes you say that, Drew?" Dad asked.

"I ran into Scott after the game," said Drew.

"How did that go?" Mom asked.

"I'm not sure. I think that he was more shocked than anything else," said Drew.

"Did he make fun of you?" Dad asked.

"Not really. He seemed more like he was mad at me because I blew him off this weekend," said Drew.

"What does that tell you?" asked Mom.

"That first he needs the shock to wear off, and then he'll start making fun of me," said Drew.

"No. What does his anger show you? You were wondering about this yesterday," said Mom

"I don't get it," said Drew.

"You were upset because you thought that you had lost a friend, and Scott was upset because he thought…"

"That he had lost a friend," said Drew. He smiled.

"Did you run into anyone else?" asked Dad.

"No one from the team," said Drew.

"But you ran into somebody," said Mom.

"Yeah," said Drew.

"Who?" asked Dad.

"Callie said 'hi' to me," said Drew. She was there because she's a volunteer coach for the sixth grade cheerleaders," said Drew.

Mom smiled.

"Did she make fun of you?" asked Dad.

"No. I tried to hide my ref hat behind my back which was probably pretty stupid," said Drew. "Now that I think about it, that was the first time we've said more than just 'hi' to each other," said Drew.

Mom hit Dad on the arm with the back of her hand. She couldn't hide the smile on her face.

"Mom!" said Drew.

"Talking to Scott must have been tough," said Dad. "In a way, though, it's good. I mean, you couldn't keep it a secret forever. Your friends were going to spot you at their little brothers' and sisters' games eventually, right?"

"Yeah," said Drew.

"Are you worried that they'll make fun of you?" asked Mom.

"I'm not worried that they will, I know that they will," said Drew.

"But when you have important decisions to make, you can't worry too much about what other people are going to think of you," said Dad.

"If I had worried too much about what others thought, then I would have never married your father," said Mom.

Dad rolled his eyes, and they laughed.

"I know," said Drew.

"Besides," said Mom. "When we were at the Murray's last night, I found out from Claire's mom that the cheerleading coach that you talked to today just broke up with her hockey player boyfriend."

"Mom!" said Drew. His cheeks flushed.

"Do you remember when we talked about this on the beach last week?" she said.

Drew nodded.

"People like you, and they want to be around you, regardless of if you're a football ref or not," said Mom.

Does Callie like me? The thought of it made Drew's cheeks red again, and he had to look down for a moment.

"So do you think that you'll stick with reffing this season?" asked Dad.

Drew was silent for a while. He didn't look up.

"What's up?" asked Dad.

There was another pause, and Drew lifted his head and said, "Ever since I was little, I wanted to be like you and play college football." Drew choked up. "I failed."

"You didn't fail," said Dad, tears welling up in his eyes. "We love you. I'm not disappointed in you at all. I'm worried about you. I don't ever again want to see you have to go through what you've been through. I don't ever want to go through it again. I want the happy, confident, healthy kid that I know and love. I just want my boy back."

"Drew," said Mom "It's hard to lose something in your life that you care deeply about, but you can't let yourself get stuck in the past. You've got to find ways to take your life back— to get back the fun, the excitement, the camaraderie. Maybe you've found one. If refereeing football can help you feel happy again, then why not go for it?"

Drew didn't say anything more. He gave his parents a hug, took the Commissioner's phone number from his Dad, and went upstairs. He sat on his bed with his phone in one hand and the phone number in the other. The game and the talk with his parents had drained him physically and emotionally. *Am I a failure? If I do this, will I lose my friends? If I do this, will Callie think that I'm a loser?* He stared at his phone, and his mind began to wander. He put the phone and the Commissioner's phone number down on his bedside table and fell asleep on top of the covers.

The next morning Drew's alarm went off. He fumbled for the off button, but he finally had to sit up to turn off the alarm clock. Drew put his head in his hands and said, "I need a three day weekend." As he got ready for school, Drew felt his stomach tighten. He knew that he should eat a good breakfast, but his fatigue and his nerves prevented it. Drew played with his food, and he wondered, *What are my friends going to say?* On the bus ride to school, Drew thought, *I just want this to be over with!* When Drew got to his locker in the freshman hallway, Scott, Troy, and Brendan were waiting for him. As he approached, Drew thought, *Practice courage.*

"Is it true?" Troy asked.

"Yes," said Drew. "You really are as dumb as you look."

The guys sniggered. "Scott's not spreading rumors. He really saw you at the Jamboree yesterday? You're really trying out to be a referee?" said Brendan.

Drew looked at Scott and said, "I thought that we went over this yesterday. I either get paid fifty bucks a game, or I get community service hours," said Drew.

"You're a *ref?*" asked Scott.

"You keep saying that," said Drew.

"Because I still can't believe it," said Scott.

"You make fifty bucks a game?" Troy asked.

"So you make one hundred and fifty bucks if you work the youth games on Sunday?" Brendan asked.

"The Commissioner doesn't think it's a good idea that I work seventh and eighth grade games because we played against some of those guys last year. I could make a hundred," said Drew.

"To watch games that you would have watched anyway," said Troy.

"Right," said Drew.

"Not bad," said Brendan.

"I think so," said Drew.

"But the uniform," said Scott.

"Yikes," said Troy.

"I know. I know. I make it look good. Scott can tell you. He saw it," said Drew. "You can borrow it if you want."

The guys sniggered again.

"But why didn't you hang out with us this weekend?" Troy asked. "Scott said you were studying the rules?"

Drew looked at the floor and didn't say anything.

"That's lame, Drew," Troy said.

"You wouldn't come to our game; you wouldn't hang out with us, and you lied to us. Ouch," said Brendan.

Just then Claire and Callie walked by. Callie said, "Hey guys."

"Hey," they said.

"Drew, are you volunteering at the football game this Sunday?" she asked.

Drew smiled. "The assignments come out tonight," he said.

"Maybe I'll see you there," Callie said.

"Ok," said Drew.

Claire bit her lip so that she wouldn't giggle.

"Bye," Callie said.

"See ya, Coach!" said Drew.

Callie and Claire turned and walked down the hall.

"Coach? She's not your coach," said Brendan.

"Her name is Callie, Drew," said Troy.

"Yeah, but she's an assistant cheerleading coach," said Drew.

"Not a good look, Drew. Not a good look," said Scott. "Neither was ditching us this weekend."

"Sorry," said Drew.

No one spoke.

"I'll see you guys at lunch?" Drew asked.

"Yeah," they said.

Drew walked to Biology class. He took his first deep breath of the day and thought, *That could have been a whole lot worse.*

When Drew got home from school that afternoon, he dropped his bag and went straight to his room to get the Commissioner's phone number. Like the night before, he sat on the edge of his bed with the phone number in one hand and his phone in the other. He stared at them for a while. He looked at the football trophies on his shelves. In the afternoon light of late summer, they shined pale gold. Drew noticed that they were dusty. He looked at the pictures, newspaper clippings, and recruiting letters that were pinned to his bulletin board. The shadows in the room hid the newspaper clippings, but Drew knew them all by heart. In his mind's eye he could hear the crowds that cheered for him, and he could hear his name announced over the stadium's speakers. *Another touchdown for Drew Hennings!* He felt sad, and he thought, *Middle school is over. I should take this stuff down.* He looked back at the phone number, sighed, and dialed.

"Hello, Commissioner MacLean? Hi, it's Drew Hennings," he said. "Yes, I would like to officiate this year." Drew listened to the Commissioner's instructions, and he said, "Yes, I'll see you Thursday." He paused and listened. "No worries. Jack will drive me…Yes, Brian gave me a rulebook last week. Thank you again for the opportunity. Bye." Drew hung up.

He changed and went for a run.

Chapter 12

DIG IT OUT

After his workout Drew showered and changed. He rubbed his hair dry with a towel, and he looked again at his football awards. Drew dropped the towel onto the back of his desk chair, and he walked downstairs. He went to the garage and got a big cardboard box. Drew returned to his room, and he cleared his desk, bulletin board, shelves, and dresser of his football awards. Dad saw the box when he got home from work. "What's all this?" he asked.

"I cleaned up," said Drew.

"I see that," said Dad.

"It was so dusty in here that I had to take my allergy medicine," said Drew.

Dad looked at the empty bulletin boards and the clean, shiny shelves and dresser top. "It looks great in here," he said.

"Thanks," said Drew. "Now I actually have space at my desk to study."

Dad saw the open football rulebook in front of Drew. "So you told the Commissioner that you wanted to ref this season?"

"Yes. I called him this afternoon," said Drew.

"I think that you made a good choice. I'm happy for you, Drew," said Dad.

"Did I just hear that Drew is going to—wow! It looks great in here, Drew," said Mom as she walked into the room.

"Thanks," said Drew. "Can I store the box in the attic?"

"Sure," said Dad.

"I forgot what your desk looked like. It's nice. And it's nice to see you using it to study. Did you do your homework?" asked Mom.

"Yes," said Drew.

"I don't know what has gotten into this boy, Mike, but we should get out of here quickly before it wears off!" said Mom.

"I guess I just don't want to get stuck in the past," said Drew.

Dad and Mom looked at each other and smiled. "I'll put the box in the attic before dinner," said Dad. He and Mom walked out of the room, and Drew continued studying the rulebook.

Six weeks flew by. Drew was busy working games every Saturday and Sunday and attending Candidates' Classes every Thursday night. To improve his officiating, Drew also started working out three times a week, and he took Jack's advice and spent at least fifteen minutes every day studying the rulebook. Drew was so busy with officiating that he had to focus more in school to make sure that he got his work done. Drew still wasn't sold on being a serious student, but his grades were better than they had ever been. The news about Drew becoming a teen ref was interesting gossip for a few days, but soon there were better stories to tell. Drew's former teammates teased him now and then, but they also asked him questions about the rules. Drew only took one Saturday off from officiating on Columbus Day weekend. It was Homecoming at Brown, and the Hennings tailgated with Dad's and Jack's old teammates. Drew was really proud that his dad had played college football, especially in the Ivy League, but Drew wondered why his Dad chose to play for the team with the ugliest uniforms in the conference, perhaps in all of college football. At Homecoming, Drew got to play a game of touch football with the Brown football alumni and their families on the rooftop field at the athletic center. Gradually, the weather got colder, the days got shorter, and the leaves turned brilliant shades of red, orange, and yellow.

It was a rainy Sunday night five days before Halloween, and Drew was thirsty. It was strange to feel thirsty when he was standing in cold New England drizzle. He recorded the timeout on his plastic scorecard. It had come as part of his football official's starter kit that Drew's parents had given him at the end of September for his fifteenth birthday, and this was the first time he had used it. *Both teams are out of timeouts*, he thought. After he put the scorecard back into his shirt pocket, he stole a glance up at the stands. *It's a decent crowd. Is Callie here?* Drew wiped the rain drops off of his watch, and he glanced at Jack.

"Bring 'em in!" Jack said. Jack was the referee, the leader of the officiating crew. Jack's white hat signified his authority, and all of the other officials wore black hats.

Drew turned towards the huddle, "We're ready to go, coaches!" The coaches hurried their final instructions to the team, and the players jogged to the center of the field. They almost ran. *I can't blame them.* Drew thought. *This is the biggest play of their season.*

Drew walked down the sideline and took his place at the line of scrimmage. When both teams made their huddles, the referee blew his whistle to signal that the ball was ready for play. Drew went through his pre-snap routine. He thought to himself: *fourth and goal on the two, three-three-three-two makes eleven.* Drew looked up at the scoreboard. There were four seconds remaining in the fourth quarter. The Duxbury Green Dragons fifth and sixth grade team was leading the Hingham Harbormen 22 to 18. The winner advanced to the youth football playoffs. *If*

I do a good job tonight, then maybe the Commish will assign me a playoff game, Drew thought. Hingham wore their home colors, red with white numbers and trim, and they had the ball.

Hingham broke the huddle, and the Duxbury defense was set and waiting for them. Drew heard cheering swell from the crowd behind him. His heart raced, and fire shot through the veins in his arms. He took a deep breath and tried to calm himself. *First step towards the goal line. First step towards the goal line.* Drew looked down the line of scrimmage at the official on the opposite sideline. The Head Linesman rolled his fists over each other several times. Drew repeated the signal.

"Know the fumbler!" said Jack, the Referee.

"Know the fumbler!" said Drew. *Rule 4. The old Oakland Raiders' "Fumblerooski"play. On fourth down only the player who fumbles the ball can recover it and advance it. If the fumble is picked up by any other player on the offense, then the play is over.*

Hingham's quarterback began his cadence, and before he finished it, the ball was snapped. It was a QB Sneak. Drew took a step towards the goal line as the offensive and defensive lines surged into one another. Drew lost sight of the quarterback in the scrum. When Drew got to the goal line, he sprinted straight for the pile looking for any sign of the ball. As he ran to the play, more and more players joined the pile. *Where was the ball? Where was the ball?* Drew's training kicked in. He had to untangle the players, find the ball and figure out who won the game. He jumped on his knees, and he heard Jack blow the whistle to stop the play. The Head Linesman echoed Jack, but the whistles didn't do much good. Players from both teams were pushing and yelling.

Drew started to "dig." He tapped players on the shoulder and said, "You're out! You're out! Play's over! You're out!" The players started to disentangle, and finally Drew caught sight of the ball. *Where was the goal line?* Even through the cold October rain, Drew could feel the sweat dripping down his forehead making his eyes sting. His throat ached from shouting, and his heart was racing, "You're out!" As the Duxbury player got up off the ground, Drew found the goal line. He looked up at the ball. The nose had crossed. "He's in! He's in!" Drew said.

Jack was standing outside of the scrum, and he faced the crowd and raised both arms. The Head Linesman did the same. The Hingham fans erupted in cheers. Drew heard cowbells clanging. *Those are obnoxious.* He looked towards the Hingham bench and saw a tidal wave of players and coaches running straight at him. He jumped to his feet and jogged to the sideline. Jack was waiting for him. It took the Head Linesman a little while to make his way through the celebration and join them.

"Great call, Drew!" said Jack as they all shook hands. Drew smiled. *It feels good,* he thought. *In fact, I haven't felt this good in a long time.*

The crew began to walk towards the exit, and the Hingham cheerleaders jogged straight at them. Drew saw Callie Walker, and he noticed that some stray ringlets of her wet hair had fallen across her cheek.

"Hey," said Drew.

After a few steps Jack said, "Who was that?"

"She's a girl from school. She's in my English class," Drew said. "We all have to do community service. Callie helps out the fifth and sixth grade cheerleaders."

The conversation stopped because the officials had reached the gate that separated the field from the stands. It was surrounded by parents from both teams, and they wanted to see that the officials had taken the game seriously. Drew picked his chin up, made sure not to make eye contact with anyone, and headed straight for the parking lot.

Chapter 13

THE MAKINGS OF A LEADER

"You did great out there tonight, kid. You've really come a long way this year. If you keep going the way you're going, the Commissioner might assign you to a playoff game," Jack said as he drove Drew home.

When they arrived at Drew's house, Jack said, "That was fun. Thanks again for working on my crew."

"No problem," said Drew. "That was fun."

"You did a heck of a job on that QB Sneak. You looked like you've been officiating for years."

"Thanks," Drew said. He looked straight ahead, and he smiled. *It would be pretty cool to work a playoff game in my first year,* he thought.

"So I'll pick you up for Thursday's Candidates' Class at 6:15p.m. sharp. Don't forget your rulebook…"

"A notebook, a pencil, and my reading glasses. Got it," said Drew.

"Good. See you then, Pal. Say 'hi' to Mom and Dad for me," Jack said.

"Will do. Thanks, Jack." Drew closed the car door and walked slowly into the house. He was tired, and his homework was waiting for him.

Monday morning on the bus ride to school, Drew took out the NCAA rulebook and tried to read it. It was written like a law book (Drew's Dad told him so), but it reminded Drew of his Geometry text. The difference was that in his math book

Drew read rules, and examples followed that helped him understand what he was reading. The rules in the football rulebook were listed in the front, and all of the examples, called Approved Rulings, were in a separate section in the back. It was dense, difficult, and dull, and the jostling and noise of the bus didn't help. Drew's head started to ache after a while, so he put the rulebook back in his bag. Jack always told him that watching a lot of football was helpful too. Watching film of college games was his favorite part of Thursday's Candidates' Class. Drew also planned to watch the Hingham JV game after school.

When the bus got to school, Drew forgot about football. He was happy to talk to his friends, and his morning classes were tough. He started in Biology lab, and he had to dissect a frog.

"Why don't we have face masks? It smells so bad!" he said to his lab partner. Drew's second period class was World History. The next period he had a Latin quiz. Drew's Latin teacher reminded him of Professor Lupin from *Harry Potter*. Drew sketched him and showed it to his friends. Over his shoulder he heard his teacher say, "A werewolf has more hair, and where is the full moon?" When the teacher moved on, Drew looked wide-eyed at his classmates, and he mouthed silently, "I told you: he's a werewolf." Geometry was fourth, and by this time Drew was getting hungry. It was a difficult class, and he had to take a lot of notes and do a lot of seatwork. However, Drew knew that if he could tough it out in math class, then he was set for the rest of the day. During the lunch block Drew had study hall. The study hall worked for thirty minutes, went to lunch for thirty minutes and came back together for another thirty minutes. Usually, when Drew got to study hall, he eased into his chair and breathed a sigh of relief. Not today. He had to get as much work done as quickly as possible so that he could go to the JV game after school. He finished his Latin homework in no time. Next, he had to work on his map of the Persian War for World History class. Drew used his textbook to find the major battles that the Greeks fought against Xerxes. He marked them on the map and connected the dots. Drew was making good progress when the lunch bell rang.

As Drew walked to the cafeteria, he thought, *It's calzones today. Maybe I'll see Callie.* He took his tray to his usual seat with the freshman football players. They were talking about last Friday's game.

"Drew, you should have seen it. We scored four touchdowns in the first half. Quincy couldn't tackle anyone. All of our touchdowns were long runs. Brendan broke a forty-yarder!" said Scott. Scott was the starting center, defensive tackle, and team Captain. His fifteenth birthday wasn't until December, and he was already five foot eleven inches and weighed two hundred and ten pounds. "If you had been playing, Drew, we would have beat them by sixty!"

"Thanks," said Drew. He looked at his food. *They mean well,* he thought. *It still feels like a punch in the gut every time they say stuff like that. But the hurt is not as bad as it used to be, and it doesn't last as long.*

"Any chance your parents will let you come back?" asked Scott.

"No. They don't want me to get too many concussions," said Drew.

"That's not fair!" said Brendan.

"But they'll let you play lacrosse in the Spring?" said Scott. "It should be your decision."

"Yeah," Drew said, and he shrugged. "I've never been taken out of a lacrosse game in an ambulance."

"That was scary," said Troy. "I thought that you were paralyzed or something."

Drew changed the subject, "Are you playing JV today?" Troy was having a great year, and there were rumors that the coaches would move him up a level.

"Yeah," said Troy.

"I wish we could have him back this week. Whitman-Hanson's going to be tough," Scott said. The Whitman-Hanson Panthers were the only challenge that stood between the Hingham freshman team and a league championship.

"Drew, are you going to watch the JVs today?" Troy asked.

"Yeah," said Drew. "I'll let you guys know what happens. Scott, Troy is still on your fantasy team, right?" The guys at the table laughed.

"You're not reffing the game are you?" he asked.

Drew hoped that the embarrassment didn't show on his face. He recovered quickly, "If I don't go, then the JVs will be missing half of their fan base." The guys laughed again. The lunch bell rang, and the boys cleaned off their table. Drew frowned and looked at his tray again so that his friends could not see his face. *I should be the one throwing Troy the ball in the JV game*, he thought. As he walked out of the cafeteria, Drew looked around for Callie.

When Drew got back to study hall, he felt ready to go. He finished his map for history, and he started on his math. He was halfway through it when the bell rang. *Good*, he thought. *Half of my math assignment and English for homework tonight. No trouble from Mom and Dad. I'm all set to go to the game.* Drew made his way to Mrs. Fitzgerald's room for English class.

Mrs. Fitzgerald had been teaching for forty years, and she had taught Drew's parents when they went to Hingham High School. When she wasn't teaching freshman English, she was the Chairwoman of the department. Each day Drew walked into her room and past her office. It looked like a closet. *I'll have to ask Dad if he ever got locked in there as a punishment.* English had never been Drew's favorite subject, but he liked Mrs. Fitzgerald. More importantly, Callie Walker was in the class. It was the only class that they took together, and Callie sat a few seats ahead of Drew. Drew took his seat in the back row and stole a glance at her. She was wearing ripped jeans and a baby blue top. Like most days, her hair was back in a ponytail. She was pretty, and she made it look effortless.

Mrs. Fitzgerald started the class with a vocabulary exercise. They were drawing pictures to help them remember synonyms and antonyms for the word *leadership.* Drew was working with *sway.* Drew rushed through his work and leaned his head against the back wall. Then he put his feet up on the desk in front of him.

Drew was just getting comfortable when he heard Claire Murray, his partner for English class, say, "Here's what I drew for antonyms. The first word that I worked with was *incompetent.*"

Drew sighed and sat up. Just then Mrs. Fitzgerald walked over to check their homework. When the teacher moved on, Drew mouthed the words "thank you" to Claire, and Claire rolled her eyes.

Next, Mrs. Fitzgerald led a class discussion on the homework questions. They talked about the end of *The Odyssey,* the part where Odysseus takes off his disguise, tells all of the bad guys that the king has returned, and then kills every last one of them. Drew made sure to raise his hand early in the discussion. *Now I can sit back and relax,* he thought. Drew put his head back and his feet up, and let his mind wander. He only tuned back in when Claire turned to him and said, "If you were Odysseus, what would *you* have done to take back your kingdom?" Drew sat up. It was the part of the lesson where Mrs. Fitzgerald had the students talk with their partners while she walked around the classroom and listened. Drew and Claire talked for what felt like a long time. When the talk in the room died down, Mrs. Fitzgerald asked some of Drew's classmates to share their solutions to Odysseus's problem.

Callie was the first to speak: "He should have asked Queen Penelope to help him get rid of the suitors. I bet that if she had just told all of them that her husband was back and that they should leave, they would have listened to her."

Scott Myers, who was also in the class, spoke next. "I wouldn't go as far as Callie. I like that Odysseus killed Antinous. He was the leader of the bad guys, and he deserved it. But I do agree with Callie that Odysseus didn't need to kill everyone. All of the suitors tried to apologize and pay him back. Why didn't he take the money and kick them out of his house? Why is Odysseus so fired up? The suitors didn't know that he was alive," Scott said.

Next, Mrs. Fitzgerald asked the students to write in their notebooks the most important lesson that they learned about leadership. When they finished, Mrs. Fitzgerald asked them to stand up and push the desks against the walls. Then she asked the students to stand in a circle in the middle of the room.

At least she lets us get up and move around a little. I wish more teachers would let us do that, Drew thought.

When the students had settled down, Mrs. Fitzgerald said, "Let's have a Closing Circle. Share with the class the most important lesson that you learned from *The Odyssey*. Who wants to go first?"

Drew was standing two students to the left of Callie. Claire, who was standing to Callie's right, volunteered to go first. Mrs. Fitzgerald instructed the class to speak in turns moving clockwise around the circle. When it was Callie's turn to speak, she said, "I learned that no leader is perfect, and that you have to learn to make mistakes, accept responsibility for them, learn from them, and move on."

Shortly afterwards it was Drew's turn to speak, and he wanted to say something that would impress Callie. *Say something smart. Say something different,* he thought. There was a pause, "Ahhh, I agree with what Callie said," was all that came out.

Mrs. Fitzgerald nodded and looked to the next speaker.

Drew said, "Mrs. Fitz!"

"Yes, Mr. Hennings," Drew could feel his cheeks turning red. "I just remembered what I wanted to say."

"Go ahead," she said.

"Courage," said Drew. "If you want to be a leader, then you have to have courage."

"Thank you, Drew," said Mrs. Fitzgerald, and she smiled.

That's great. She's laughing at me. What a stupid answer! thought Drew.

Shortly afterwards, Scott spoke, and he said, "I learned that a great leader assembles a great team of people to help him accomplish his goals."

Drew couldn't help stealing a quick glance at Callie. She was looking at Scott and nodding her head in agreement.

Why didn't I think of that one! Drew thought.

When the Closing Circle was over, the class put the desks back in rows and wrote down the homework in their agenda books, study for a test on *The Odyssey* on Wednesday. They were just finished when the bell rang. As Drew walked to gym class he thought, *Maybe I could ask Callie if she wants to study for the test at the library tomorrow?*

Gym class went by in a flash because they played volleyball, and Drew loved it. When the match was over, he changed in the locker room, the bell rang, and he went out to the football field to watch the JV game.

Chapter 14

THE THREE-AND-ONE PRINCIPLE

Drew sat at midfield in the last row of bleachers. While the teams warmed up, Drew took out his rulebook and read a part of Rule 10 called "Enforcement Procedures." Drew learned from his referee classes that when a player commits a penalty, it is very important to know where the penalty happened and where the play ended. Drew read the rules and tried to summarize them in his own words: *If the offense commits a holding or blocking penalty behind the line of scrimmage, then enforce the penalty at the spot where the play began.* Next, Drew read the "Three-and-One Principle," and he tried to summarize it. He focused on this section because Jack told him that officials used the "Three-and-One Principle" all of the time. *If the play ends beyond the line of scrimmage, and there is a penalty, then three things can happen. The "one" is the place where the ball is located when the play ends. The "three" are the possible ways that officials could enforce a penalty. If the defensive team commits a penalty, then the refs add yards to the end of the run. It doesn't matter where the penalty happened. If the offensive team commits a foul, then it matters where the penalty happened. If the penalty happened ahead of where the football is at the end of the play, then the refs go to the football and take yards away. If the penalty happened between where the play ended and where the play began, then the refs go to that spot and enforce the penalty from there.*

The rule was difficult to remember, but Drew's Dad had helped him learn it last Saturday morning. They were sitting at

146

the kitchen table, and Drew's Dad had told him to search his closet for his old football toy, a box full of red and blue plastic players and a football field made of green felt. Drew went upstairs and dug the dusty toy out of the back of his closet. When he came back downstairs, his Dad was waiting for him, and he had a yellow poker chip in his hand.

They set up the football figurines, and Dad said, "I remember that when you were little, you used to play with this for hours."

Drew smiled. "That was a long time ago," he said.

"Sometimes it feels like that; sometimes it feels like it was yesterday," said his Dad. "Have the running back run up the middle and get tackled."

Drew did as he was told, and he added in sound effects just like the ones that he used when he was little. Drew's Dad laughed. When the toy running back was tackled, Dad said, "There was a flag on the offense here," and he placed the yellow poker chip ahead of the running back. "What do you do?"

Drew thought for a moment, and he said, "Start at the end of the run, and push them back."

"Correct. What about if the offense committed a penalty here?" Dad said, and he placed the yellow poker chip between the running back and his teammates who were still lined up in their original places.

"Enforce the penalty from the spot of the foul," said Drew.

"Good," said Dad. "What would happen if the offense committed a holding penalty at or behind the line of scrimmage?" He placed the poker chip there.

"Enforce the penalty from where the play began, the original line of scrimmage," said Drew.

"Well done," said Dad. Next, he flicked the poker chip up in the air like he was flipping a coin. It bounced off of the table and knocked down several players.

"What was that?" Drew asked.

"It was my version of a penalty on the defense. The defensive end knew Kung Fu, and he knocked out a bunch of guys," said Dad.

Drew laughed, and he said, "Where did it happen?"

"Does it matter?" Dad asked.

"It always matters," said Drew.

"True, but is it going to change how you enforce the penalty?" Dad asked.

"I get what you're saying. No. The penalty could be anywhere. We're going to add yardage to the end of the run," said Drew.

"Good thinking, kid," Dad said.

"Thanks," said Drew. "So where in the book is the rule for excessive use of martial arts?" Dad and Drew laughed.

Just then Libby and Mom came into the kitchen, and Libby said, "Look, Mom: they're sharing their toys so nicely!"

"My two little boys," said Mom.

Drew's flashback ended as the Hingham and Silver Lake JV teams lined up for the opening kickoff. His stomach felt a little tight, and his hands were sweaty. *When I played, I used to feel like this before every kickoff,* he thought. However, today it was not the fear of getting hit that made him nervous, it was the fear of embarrassing himself because he forgot the rules. *You know this stuff,* he thought. *It's easier to see it in a game than it is to read about it. That's why you're here.*

The game started. Hingham was in red and white with a red H on their helmets. They were playing the Silver Lake Lakers who wore silver and white with red trim. Hingham drove right down the field. Drew watched Troy play receiver. No passes came his way, but his blocking was solid. He was playing aggressively too. *That looks like so much fun,* Drew thought.

When Hingham was on the Lakers' thirty-yard line, Drew saw the first penalty flag of the game. Drew watched the referee signal with a hand in front of his face that pretended to grab a facemask. Next, the referee pointed to Silver Lake. Drew tested himself. *I know what happened: a Silver Lake player grabbed the running back's facemask. It happened at the end of the run at the 30-yard line. According to the "Three and One Principle," if the defense fouls, then add the penalty to the end of the run.* Drew knew that the penalty was fifteen yards, and he did some quick math. *Hingham should get the ball at the 15-yard line, first down and ten yards to go.* Drew watched the referee pick up the ball, walk it to the fifteen-yard line, and put it on the ground. *I was right!*

A few plays later Troy caught a fade pass in the corner of the end zone. Drew's first instinct was to cheer for Troy. As he clapped he thought, *I should have been the one throwing him that pass.* Even though he was jealous of the JV quarterback, Drew continued to cheer loudly. *Practice courage,* he thought to himself. Hingham went for two on the extra point, but they got stopped at the goal line. Drew watched closely as the official on the Hingham sideline, the Line Judge, sprinted along the goal line to make the call. *I did that yesterday!* Drew thought. Silver Lake rallied in the second quarter, but as time expired in the second half, their drive stalled. At halftime Hingham lead 6-0.

Drew walked down the bleachers and onto the field. The teams were huddled with their coaches in either end zone. The officials were sitting on the Hingham bench near midfield. "Looks great from up top, fellas!" Drew said as he shook hands with all three of them.

"Good to see you again, John," said Drew.

"Hey, Drew!" John said. "How is the Candidates' Class going?"

"Good," Drew said. "But I learn just as much from working flag football games with you."

"I'm glad to hear it. I can teach, and you can run. This partnership might keep me officiating for a few more years!" said John.

"That sounds good to me," said Drew.

"So what brings you here? If I had known, then I could have put you on the chain crew. It would have been nice to have someone who knows what he's doing," said John.

Drew anticipated this. The chain crew was three volunteers who carried the down marker and the stakes up and down the sideline during the game. They helped the referees count the downs, keep track of the line of scrimmage, and mark the line to gain for first downs. Working on a chain crew was a great way to watch a game and learn how to be a ref, and Drew had worked on several chain crews during seventh and eighth grade youth games. However, the last thing Drew wanted was to be seen carrying the chains for the Hingham JV team. He could imagine their comments, "He used to be pretty good. Why isn't he playing this year?" Drew could handle being embarrassed in public, but pity would be too much to take.

"It's hard to carry the chains and look at the rulebook at the same time," Drew said without making eye contact with anyone. "I figured that I would study the book, watch the game, and be ready just in case I get a call to work a youth football playoff game," said Drew.

"Good man," said John, and he smiled. John turned to the others and said, "I've said it from the beginning. I like this kid. I know that he's too young, but why not take a chance on him?"

The other officials nodded in agreement, and John said, "Drew, I can help you with your referee education. I had an interesting play in my varsity game this weekend." Sharing stories was another way that officials learned the rules, and Drew enjoyed listening to them. John continued, "I was working a varsity game between Brockton and Xaverian,"

Drew's mouth opened. Brockton was one of the biggest schools in the state, and they had a long history of great football. Drew tried to imagine what reffing a game between Brockton and Xaverian would be like with a huge crowd of rowdy fans. He realized his mouth was hanging open. He closed it, and tuned back in to John's story.

"The receiver was standing in the front of the end zone. He jumped to catch a long pass. When he was airborne, his foot hit the pylon. He reached his arms out in front of him, caught the ball, came down with both feet in the end zone, and was immediately pushed out of bounds. When he went out of bounds, the football was at the ½ yard line. What da'ya got?"

"First and goal at the half yard line!" said Drew. He answered like he was racing through a problem in Geometry class. John frowned and shook his head. An awkward silence followed. The other two officials didn't want to risk the embarrassment of a wrong answer.

"Rule 4. Is the pylon in bounds or out of bounds?" asked John.

"It's out of bounds," said Drew.

"Can a receiver catch a pass with one foot out of bounds?"

"No."

"So what's the call?"

"Incomplete pass," said Drew.

"Thata boy!" said John.

"I'll bet the coach didn't like that call," said one of the other officials.

"It took some explaining," said John. He shrugged and smiled.

Drew's stomach dropped at the thought of it. *There is no way I could make a call like that in a game. Even if I did get it right, how would I explain it to an angry coach?* he thought.

"Should we get back to it?" said John.

Drew took his place back in the stands, and the game resumed. The teams kept trading punts. The defenses played okay, but the offenses were disorganized. *That's what happens when you spend the whole week on scout team running someone else's offense,* Drew thought. Slowly, Silver Lake gained field position and momentum. By the middle of the fourth quarter, they finally had a chance to tie the game. The running back took a handoff into the line, but there was nowhere to go. He ran for the right sideline with a defender right behind him. The back turned on a burst of speed and escaped. As he neared the sideline he turned upfield. There was only one defender between him and the end zone. The defender was fighting off a block from the wide receiver. Just as the defender escaped the block, the receiver grabbed his jersey. The defender lost his balance giving the running back just enough time to sprint past him and into the end zone.

That's a hold! Drew thought. John and the Line Judge thought so too. They both threw their flags. Drew started to think about how to enforce the penalty, and he was surprised to notice that the Line Judge was running towards the goal line. *What is he doing? The play doesn't count. Wait. The play's not over. The play's not over. Jack always tells me: officiate the whole play.* The official reached the goal line pylon and signaled touchdown, but the Silver Lake crowd was silent. As the officials huddled, Drew tested himself. *What happened? Silver Lake held. When did it happen? During the run. Where did it happen?* Drew looked for the yellow flag on the field. It was on the ground where the play started. Looking down on the play from the bleachers reminded Drew of when his Dad had used action figures and a poker chip to help him study Rule 10. *Ok. It's just like what Dad and I worked on in the kitchen. The holding happened at the yard-line where the play began. The "Three and One Principle" says that if the run ends beyond the line of scrimmage, and the penalty happens where the play began, then I enforce the penalty from where the play began. The play began on the twelve-yard line, and holding is a ten yard penalty. Twelve plus ten is twenty-two. The next play will be from the twenty-two-yard line.* Drew finished the mental math as the officials were placing the ball on the twenty-two-yard line. Drew had solved the problem correctly, and he was happy about it. *Now all I have to do is get it right during a playoff game, if I get the chance to ref a playoff game.*

Hingham's defense held, and they won the game. Afterwards, Drew texted his Mom and asked for a ride home. Then he went down to the field and congratulated the officials, "See you at the meeting on Thursday!" said Drew. Meanwhile, Troy had just finished shaking hands with the players from Silver Lake. *Practice courage,* thought Drew. He pointed at Troy and said, "Heck of a catch, Troy!" Troy smiled. Drew gave him a thumbs up and walked to the parking lot.

Chapter 15
STUDY SESSION

Drew worked hard during study hall on Tuesday, and he finished his math homework by the time the lunch bell rang. He sat with his football friends. "That touchdown catch was sick, Troy. Congrats," said Drew.

"Did it look as good live as it did on YouTube?" asked Scott.

"Thanks for being there, Drew," said Troy. "Wish you could've been the one throwing the ball."

It was a very kind and classy thing to say, but to Drew it felt like another knife in the heart. *Practice courage*, he reminded himself. "Thanks," said Drew. "It's tough." The words fell out of Drew's mouth before he could stop them.

"What does *that* mean?" asked Scott.

Drew looked startled. His friends were staring at him and waiting for him to speak. "Forget it," he said.

"Not happening," said Scott.

"I just meant—" said Drew.

"That it's hard for you to cheer for your friends," said Brendan.

"That's not what I meant…" said Drew.

"What did you mean?" asked Troy.

Drew took a deep breath. He said, "What I really meant was—I miss playing football with you guys, and it's tough to watch you play without me."

"Oh," said Scott.

"I let you guys down. It's—" said Drew.

155

"Difficult," said Troy. "I get it. When I play on the freshman team, I play every snap of the game. Now that I'm on JV, I only play on offense. I hate sitting there and watching the older guys having all of the fun. I get annoyed, and I'm playing in the game. I get it."

"Remember during hockey when I was on the penalty kill and took that wrist shot to the knee?" said Brendan.

"Yeah," said Drew.

"I had to sit out for two weeks. My parents made me go to every practice. I even went to the 5 a.m. ones. It was so boring. I hated it," said Brendan.

"You've always had my back, Drew," said Scott. "I'll always have yours, even if you wear zebra stripes."

Drew looked at his friends and smiled. "You can borrow my ref shirt any time, Scott," Drew said.

"I don't know. It'd be pretty tight," said Scott.

"The girls would love it," said Drew.

"Funny you should mention that," said Troy. "Have you guys noticed that Callie says 'hi' to Drew in the hallway a lot? Is it because of the ref uniform?"

"No doubt. Absolutely," said Brendan. The guys laughed.

"She almost never talked to you last year," said Scott. "Maybe Troy is right."

"She had a boyfriend last year," said Brendan.

"I've reffed a couple Hingham games, and I see Callie there," said Drew. "We talk sometimes."

"So you're saying that it's the uniform." said Troy.

"Definitely the stripes," said Brendan.

"They're hot right now," said Scott.

"It could be a good costume idea for the Halloween Dance. Are you guys in?" asked Drew.

"No," said Scott.

"Never," said Brendan.

"Not a chance," said Troy.

"Will you guys even be back from the Whitman-Hanson game in time for the dance?" asked Drew.

"I think so," said Scott.

"Are you excited for Whitman-Hanson?" Drew asked.

Troy thought for a moment and said, "The thing is I'm still sore from the Silver Lake game. The coaches never give JV a day off. I wish I were back on the freshman team with you guys."

"That makes two of us!" said Scott.

When lunch was over, Drew tried to look for Callie, but she was already gone. *She talks to you because she feels bad for you,* he thought. *If I hadn't gotten hurt, then everything would be different.* As he walked back to study hall, Drew daydreamed about wearing his game jersey again.

He'd walk Callie back to class. When they passed the posters for the dance, she would say, "You're taking me to the dance, right?"

Just then one of the varsity players would call out, "Hey, Drew! Coach needs to see you before practice. Something about suiting up with the varsity this weekend as a back-up QB. Make sure you go to his office right after school."

The day dream ended when Drew got back to study hall, and saw his World History homework lying unfinished on the desk. *Back to reality,* he thought. Drew borrowed a textbook, read the pages that his teacher had assigned for homework, and answered the guided reading questions at the end of the chapter.

He wanted all of his homework done so that he had time after school to put his plan into action. He had just checked off his World History homework in his agenda book when the bell rang. *Practice courage,* he told himself. *The worst that can happen is that she says 'no.' It wouldn't be any different than right now.* It was time to go to English class, a chance for Drew to see Callie.

When he arrived at Mrs. Fitzgerald's room, the desks were already arranged in groups of four. Each group had a number written on computer paper and taped to the center of it. The teacher was standing beside her desk, greeting the students and handing a playing card to each one. A small line formed in front of her. While he waited, Drew looked for Callie. She was seated in group five. She wore dark jeans, a black v-neck top, and a pink and orange scarf. Her hair was down. Drew recognized that she didn't wear it like that very often.

"Good afternoon, Mr. Hennings." Mrs. Fitzgerald's greeting startled Drew. She handed him a playing card.

"Thank you, Mrs. Fitz," said Drew. He flipped the card over, and it was four of diamonds. He looked up, and saw Claire sitting at group four. Drew made his way over and took his seat.

"Hey, Claire."

"Hi, Drew," she said.

Mrs. Fitzgerald called the class to attention. They were playing review games to prepare for tomorrow's test on *The Odyssey*, and their homework was to study. Mrs. Fitzgerald had a SmartBoard, and she made review games for her students to play. The groups worked together to answer questions about plot, characters, and vocabulary. Mrs. Fitzgerald rewarded them with Starbursts.

When it came time to review the meanings of important quotes and to prepare for the essay portion of the test, Mrs. Fitzgerald reshuffled the groups, "Each of your cards has a suit, diamonds, clubs, spades, or hearts," she explained. "If your card has a club on it, then please join your new group by the door. If your card has a heart on it, then please meet in the back of the room by the computers. If your card has a diamond on it, then please meet by the windows, and if your card has a spade on it, then please meet at the front of the room near my desk."

Drew hoped that Callie would be in his new group, but she was not. The only good thing was that Scott was in the diamonds group with Drew, and it was good to sit in the sun by the windows. When the students moved to their new groups and arranged their desks in a circle, Mrs. Fitzgerald gave them their assignment. First, she would display a quote on the SmartBoard, and the group had to analyze it.

"Put the quote in your own words, identify the figurative language, and explain the figurative language," she said. Then Mrs. Fitzgerald displayed the phrase, "the strategist Odysseus."

Drew looked across the room at Callie's group. *She was looking at me! Ok. Focus. Say something smart,* he thought. "That describes Odysseus," said Drew.

"Really, genius? Is that why his name is part of the quote?" said Scott.

"Seriously, Scott. It's one of those descriptive things...They remind you who the characters are...it begins with "e"...epithet! It's an epithet!" said Drew. He made sure not to look at Callie.

Scott followed Drew's lead, and he said, "That happened in the chapter when we first met him."

Drew added: "He was breaking up with Calypso, but he didn't want to make her mad…"

Scott broke in "…because he wanted to use her to help him get home!"

Mrs. Fitzgerald walked by and overheard them. She asked Scott to summarize their analysis for the class. When he finished, she asked Drew a follow-up question, "What does this teach you about leadership?"

"A good leader has to be smart," he said.

Mrs. Fitzgerald smiled, and she said, "Well done, gentlemen." Next, she put a handful of Starbursts on the desks of the diamond group.

"It's gonna rain Starbursts over here!" said Scott.

The class laughed, and he and Drew slapped five. Drew stole a glance at Callie, but she was busy talking to her group. *Did she notice?* Then the doubts returned. *You're not a quarterback anymore. She's not interested,* he thought.

The game continued, and Drew and Scott won a few more Starbursts. After offering many quotes to the class, most were Homeric Similes, Mrs. Fitzgerald prepared the students for the essay portion of the test.

"I won't tell you the prompt before the test, but talk with your groups and try to guess the question. When you come up with a good question, simulate brainstorming an answer to it. How would you answer? What would be the main idea of your essay? What text evidence would you use to support your answer?"

The groups got to work, and the room got loud. Even though class was coming to an end, Drew was determined to try and impress Callie. He stayed focused, but he and Scott could not resist having a little fun too.

"How many girlfriends can you have before your wife breaks up with you?" said Drew.

"How much wine can a Cyclops drink before he passes out?" said Scott.

Mrs. Fitzgerald closed the lesson. The class put the desks back in rows and packed up their books. Drew started to get nervous. *Give it up. She doesn't like you,* he thought. His palms were sweaty, and his stomach tightened. Drew saw Callie in line near the door. *Practice courage,* he thought. He tried to move closer to where she was standing. The bell rang, and the class emptied into the hallway. Drew hurried down the hall until he was walking beside her.

"Callie, hey, uh, any chance you want to study for the test with me? I was going to the library after school. Do you want to go?"

She hesitated. "I don't know. I'll think about it. I gotta go to class. Maybe I'll see you later, ok?"

"Yeah," said Drew. His heart was racing, and his cheeks felt like they were on fire. *"I'll think about it." Really? Come on! You "took the L" on that one, Drew,* he thought. Then he thought, *Who saw that?* He listened, but he didn't hear anybody making fun of him. Drew did not look around. He kept his eyes focused on the end of the hallway, and he walked to gym class.

The gym teacher let his students run laps around the track if they did not want to play the game that he was teaching. Drew wanted to run. He needed to run. His original plan was to keep in good shape in case he got the chance to ref a playoff game this weekend. Now he was hurt and embarrassed, and he needed an outlet. Drew warmed up with the class and started to jog. His early pace was way too fast. Drew ran as if he were in a race, but his mind stopped racing and so did his feet. He eventually settled into a good pace. Drew ran three miles, walked some warm-down laps, and did some cool-down stretches. The run made him feel better. He went inside and changed, and the bell rang to end the day. Drew was still sweaty, but he didn't care. He just wanted to go to his locker and go home. As he approached his locker, Drew could see Claire waiting for him. She had her back to him, and she was talking to someone. Drew frowned. *She heard what happened, and she feels sorry for me,* he thought. As he got closer, Drew saw that she was talking to Callie.

Chapter 16

GOOD NEWS

Drew took a deep breath and tried to be brave. "Hey, Callie. Hi, Claire," he said.

"I told Claire about studying for the English test at the library. Can she come with us?" Callie said.

"Ahhh...Yeah, sure," said Drew. *Callie didn't say "yes." I'm confused*, thought Drew.

Drew saw Claire frown, and she recoiled like he had insulted her. Drew's heart began to race. The seconds dragged by in agonizing silence. *Practice courage*, he said to himself. Drew looked Claire in the eyes, "I'm sorry. Of course you can come with us. I didn't mean to be rude. I thought that Callie said 'no.' I was surprised. That's all," said Drew.

Callie broke in: "I thought about it, and I want to study with you."

The words sent a surge of adrenaline through Drew, and his hands tingled. He exhaled, smiled, and said, "Cool."

Claire smirked and looked away.

"I can't stay too long," said Callie. "I have to coach cheerleading at 4:30 p.m."

"Then let's go," said Drew.

The three walked out of the school and down School Street to Main Street. It was another warm, sunny afternoon. *It was a good thing that I put on deodorant after gym class,* Drew thought. The leaves crunched under their feet, but the trees were still full of color. Claire, Callie, and Drew talked about school and teachers, and Callie talked about the funny things that her cheer-leaders did. The ten-minute walk to the library flew by. *Just the walk was worth it,* thought Drew.

When they got to the library, Claire suggested that they use one of the study rooms on the first floor. Claire walked right up to the circulation desk and asked the librarian if the room was available. Claire wrote her name on the sign-in sheet, and the librarian gave her the key. The study room was a narrow rectangle with a glass wall that looked out on the library. Inside there was a big table, four chairs, and a white board. When they got to the room, they dropped their bags.

"Do you guys want waters?" asked Drew.

"Sure. Thanks. We'll be right back," said Claire.

Drew got the waters from the vending machine in the lobby, and he came back to the study room. He took out his binder, book, a pen, and his phone. *You must really like this girl, Drew. You're in a library, and you're doing your homework right after school!* he thought. Then he thought, *I wonder what Claire and Callie are talking about?*

When the girls returned, they took out their books and note-books. The three got to work. Drew knew that Callie was good at English, and he really wanted to impress her. He had never studied so hard for a test in his life. They quizzed each other on characters, plot, and vocabulary words. They took turns guessing what quotes Mrs. Fitzgerald would put on the exam, and they tested each other to see who could come up with the best explanation. A half hour went by quickly. Finally, they studied for the essay.

"What do you think Mrs. Fitz is going to ask us?" said Claire.

"It's going to be something about leadership," said Callie.

"It's all we ever talked about," said Drew.

"Do you think Odysseus was a good leader or a bad one?" asked Claire.

"The prompt will be something like that," said Callie.

"I agree," said Drew.

Callie looked at Drew and said, "How would you answer the question?"

At first he was startled, but he rose and turned toward the whiteboard. He hoped that they did not see his cheeks turn red. *Get a grip, Hennings!* he thought. Drew took the black dry erase marker and tried to write. Nothing happened.

"Here. Use one of mine," said Claire.

Of course she has extra markers. I'm surprised she didn't ask me what color I wanted to use. It's like studying with Hermione Granger. "Thanks," said Drew. In blue marker he wrote the words "good + bad" in the center of the board and circled them. The move gave him time to think. Then he wrote the words "Calypso," "Cyclops," and "Fight with Suitors." Next, Drew wrote a "+" over "Calypso." He turned to Callie and Claire, "I think that Odysseus was a good leader when he broke up with Calypso because he used her to help him get home to his family."

"But he called Penelope ugly, and he cheated on her for years. How is that being a good leader?" asked Callie.

Drew didn't have an answer.

"Finish your thought, Drew," said Claire.

Drew moved on, "I think that Odysseus was both a good leader and a bad one during the fight with the Cyclops." He wrote a "+" and a "-" on the white board. "He never should have waited at the cave for the Cyclops to come back. That was stupid, but once they were trapped, Odysseus stayed calm and came up with a good plan to get his men out."

"How could he have known what the Cyclops was going to do?" said Claire.

"Yeah, but he took a risk, and he didn't need to," said Callie.

I can't say anything right. She's tough, Drew thought. *At least I've got Callie's attention.* He continued, "Odysseus was a good leader in his fight with the suitors. He took time to learn about the situation before he started the fight, and he was smart to take the suitors' weapons away and lock the doors so that they could not escape or get help." Drew tossed the marker back to Claire and sat down. Callie got up next and borrowed a red marker from Claire. Callie added Scylla and Charybdis to the graphic organizer. *Why didn't I think of that one?* thought Drew.

Callie said, "Odysseus obviously made the right choice because all of his men could have been killed, but they only lost six. So he was a good leader, but I think that he could have done better."

"I agree," said Drew.

"Is that all that you ever say?" Claire asked. "How could he have done better?"

"He could have told his men the truth. They could have helped him fight Scylla," said Callie.

"Wasn't it a prophecy that at least six would die? Mortals can't change those things," said Drew. He stuck his tongue out at Claire.

Claire hit Drew with her elbow. "Wouldn't they get scared and mutiny?" she asked.

"I don't think so," Callie replied. "They had fought for Odysseus for a really long time. They were loyal, and they knew how to win battles. You're right Drew, maybe six men would have died anyway, but at least they would have died fighting. It would have taken a little courage for Odysseus to make the decision to tell his crew about the monster and whirlpool, but didn't you say in class that a leader has to have courage?"

I can't believe she remembered what I said, Drew thought.

"Drew?" said Claire.

"Right," said Drew. "I agree."

"You said it again!" said Claire.

"What? She made a good point. What do you want me to say?" said Drew.

They all laughed.

Claire followed Callie, and she wrote in purple, her favorite color. Claire added Nausicaa, Athena, and Penelope to the board. "Why do we only think about the boys?" she asked. "Without Athena, Odysseus would be trapped on Calypso's island or drowned by Poseidon. Penelope ran Ithaca by herself for twenty years, and she came up with two clever plans to delay getting remarried. Women can be great leaders too."

Those kinds of details will really impress Mrs. Fitz, thought Drew. When Claire was finished, all three of them took pictures of the board with their phones. *I got to look at this again in study hall tomorrow,* thought Drew. They texted their parents for rides, packed their things, returned the key, and went outside.

It was cool outside. Callie, Claire, and Drew had talked themselves out, and no one said very much. *This should be awkward, but it's not. I liked talking about the book, and I liked being with Callie. I'm glad that I asked her. It was worth it,* thought Drew. A car pulled up, but it wasn't Drew's Mom. It was Jack.

"Where's Mom?" asked Drew.

"She's at home," said Jack

"Hey, Mr. MacDonald," said Claire.

"Hi, Claire! Thanks for babysitting Drew," said Jack.

"No problem," she said.

I never hear Jack called by his last name, thought Drew. "Jack, this is Callie Walker. She was the coach of the Hingham cheerleaders at the Duxbury game that we reffed on Sunday," said Drew.

"It's nice to meet you, Callie."

"It's nice to meet you too," said Callie.

"Drew's mom told me you were studying for an English test. Callie, Claire: I have to congratulate you. This may be the first time that Drew has ever studied for a test," said Jack.

"Come on," said Drew.

"I think he'll do fine," said Callie.

Drew could feel his cheeks get red again.

"You mean he didn't slow you down or distract you or anything like that?"

"No," said the girls.

"It's a miracle!" said Jack. Next Jack said, "Drew, are you done with all of your homework?"

"Yeah," said Drew.

"I just got a call from the Commissioner. He asked me if I wanted to get a crew together and work a make-up game in Marshfield. You interested?"

"But my gear is at the house, I—"

"Your gear is in my car. I dropped by your house, and your Mom gave me your bag. Can you help me?"

"Sure," said Drew. "Bye, Claire. Bye, Callie. Thanks."

"See you at school tomorrow," said Callie.

"Good luck, Drew," said Claire.

Drew got in Jack's car, and he thought, *They don't tease me at all for being a referee. I guess they look at it like coaching cheerleading or volunteering at the animal shelter.*

As Jack and Drew headed for the brand new stadium at Marshfield High School, Drew felt like he was leaving the girls early to go do something important. For the first time he actually felt a little bit proud of being a football official.

Chapter 17

OBVIOUS INTENT

"Who are they playing?" asked Drew as the car headed down Main Street towards Route 3A South.

"Bridgewater," said Jack.

"Two good teams," said Drew.

"Should be a good game."

"Thanks for thinking of me," said Drew.

"Don't mention it. We'll talk more about the game later. Tell me about Callie."

"Just a girl from school," said Drew.

"Is she *a* girl, or is she *the* girl?" asked Jack.

"I don't know yet," said Drew. He smiled and looked down. Drew didn't want Jack to see his face.

Jack was silent for a while. "How's Claire? I haven't seen her since the Fourth of July party at your parent's."

"I didn't see her much this summer either. She went to camp in New Hampshire. A place called Takodah," said Drew.

"Is she still smarter than you?"

"Yup," said Drew.

"You were smart to ask her to study with you. Is she good friends with Callie?" asked Jack.

"They're not best friends, but…" *Why was she there?* Drew wondered. *Did Claire have to convince Callie to say "yes"? Is that Callie's way of saying that she just wants to be friends?*

"You were saying?" said Jack.

"Yeah. Sorry. They're friends. We got a lot of work done. I'm glad that I went," said Drew.

"Good. Let's talk a little football?"

Drew was relieved.

"You did well last game. You'll work the same position tonight. If there is a run to your side, then you determine where the run ends. If there is a pass to your side, go downfield. If a run play goes out of bounds, remember to mark the spot where the play ended with your foot and turn to watch the players who ran into the sideline. These are fifth and sixth graders, so there probably won't be any trouble on the sidelines. If you think that there could be trouble, then drop one of your bean bags to mark the spot of the ball, and get in there to break things up. I'll keep the game clock, and I'll update you near the end of the quarter and the end of the half. What rules did you study this week?"

"Ten. I studied the Three-and-One Principle," said Drew.

"Good," said Jack. "Always check my math when we walk off a penalty, and I want you to walk with me."

"Got it," said Drew.

The pregame conference went on for a little while longer, and then Jack and Drew were silent for the final minutes of the drive. Drew looked out the window. *I like the quiet. It helps me focus,* he thought. As they approached the school, Drew could see the light towers shining with a pretty sunset behind them. Drew's heartbeat sped up, and his stomach turned. He took a breath to steady himself.

The field was new, and it was beautiful. The stands were surprisingly small. Drew changed quickly in the locker room and joined Jack at midfield for the coin toss. Drew started to shiver a little. He was chilly but excited. *I love the adrenaline rush I get before a game,* he thought. As soon as the ball was kicked, Drew felt like himself again. Marshfield, dressed in green helmets with a white M, green jerseys and black pants, marched right down the field. Bridgewater, dressed in black pants, red jerseys, and red helmets with a badger logo, answered on the next drive. At the end of the first quarter, the score was tied at eight. The teams traded punts in the second quarter. Near the half, Bridgewater had another good chance to score. They drove all the way to the Marshfield thirty-five-yard line. With six seconds remaining, Bridgewater called timeout. Drew met Jack in the middle of the field.

Jack said, "They're going to pass. Remember: if the pass is to your side, get downfield so that you can have a good look at the play. Let's call the players back in."

Drew told the coaches that the timeout was over, and he took his place on the sideline. Jack blew his whistle to signal that the ball was ready for play, and Bridgewater jogged to the line of scrimmage.

Drew went through his pre-snap routine, *Third down and six at the thirty-five. The line to gain is the twenty-nine. This will be the last play of the half.*

The quarterback took the snap and rolled to Drew's side of the field. Drew took a few shuffle steps, turned ninety-degrees and started to run downfield. He watched a Bridgewater receiver stutter step and sprint by the Marshfield defensive back. The receiver was several steps ahead when he started to slow down. His eyes were glued to the sky. He planted his downfield foot and tried to run back towards the quarterback.

The ball is in the air. The throw is too short, thought Drew.

The defender ran right at the receiver and tackled him. The ball hit the Marshfield player in the back while the receiver tried desperately to reach around him and catch the ball.

That's pass interference! The defender tackled the receiver while the ball was in the air. He didn't even look at the ball. Drew reached for his belt, grabbed his flag, and threw it towards the players on the ground. The flag landed about three yards short of his target. Drew continued to jog towards the players. When he reached the flag on the ground, he picked it up and tossed it underhand to the yard line where the penalty occurred. Drew blew his whistle loudly three times. He turned and waited for Jack.

Jack jogged towards him, and Drew decided to meet him half way. "What do you got?" asked Jack.

"Defensive Pass Interference. The defender tackled the receiver while the ball was in the air. He didn't even look back to see where the ball was," said Drew.

"Is your flag where the penalty happened?"

"Yes," said Drew.

"It was 'obvious intent to impede' by the defender?" asked Jack.

That's a direct quote from Rule Seven, thought Drew, "Yes."

"So we've got DPI, and it's deep downfield, so we are going to go fifteen yards from the original line of scrimmage and give Bridgewater a first down. That was the last play of the half—"

"What do we do? Does the half end?" said Drew.

"Whoa. Calm down. Think. You can't end a half on a penalty. Bridgewater is going to have an untimed down."

"Got it," said Drew.

"Can you please go get the football so that the game can continue?" asked Jack.

"Yeah. Sorry," Drew sprinted after the ball. By the time he had thrown the ball to Jack, Jack had already marched off the penalty. The ball was on the twenty-yard line.

Bridgewater used their play to throw one more pass. This time the quarterback rolled out to Jack's side before he threw. The pass was incomplete, and the half ended in a tie.

Jack and Drew got sports drinks at the snack shack, and they returned to midfield.

"Drew, you have to officiate the whole play. You can't stop when you see a penalty. You forgot to signal 'incomplete pass.'"

"It's just so much to—" Drew caught himself. "Sorry. See the whole play. Got it."

The second half started. Marshfield's defense held. When they got the ball back, they took it down the field and scored. They missed the extra point, and the score was 14-8. Drew felt good. He was focused, and his mechanics were becoming second nature. *I've got the best seat in the house to watch a football game. This is great!* he thought.

As the fourth quarter began, Drew began to lose focus. He was hungry and tired. Bridgewater drove deep into Marshfield territory, but with just a few minutes left, they fumbled. Drew knew what to do. He sprinted to the middle of the field. When he got there, he searched for the ball. It didn't take him long, "Green's got it, Jack! Green ball!" said Drew. *Never signal the direction. You might get turned around in the pile,* he reminded himself.

Jack signaled, and the home crowd cheered. Marshfield gained two first downs and ran out the clock. When Jack and Drew walked off the field, Jack saw the Commissioner.

"Good game, fellas," the Commissioner said.

"Thanks, Commish!" said Jack.

Commissioner MacLean looked at Drew, "This young man looked pretty good out there," he said.

Jack said, "His mechanics have progressed, and he's working hard to learn the rules."

"Thanks," said Drew.

"Have you been to every Candidates' Class?" asked the Commissioner.

"Yes," said Drew.

"Are you going to the class on Thursday?" he asked.

"Yes," Drew replied.

Jack broke in, "I drive Drew to the meetings. He asks a lot of good questions."

"Good." Commissioner MacLean paused then went on, "I was thinking of having four man crews for the playoff games on Sunday. Drew, do you want to work on Jack's crew for the fifth and sixth grade playoff game?"

"Yes! Thank you!" said Drew.

The Commissioner smiled. "You did a good job out there tonight. Don't forget to get paid over at the snack shack. I'll see you on Thursday."

"Yes, sir," said Drew. They all shook hands.

Jack and Drew went to the snack shack, and the President of Marshfield Youth Football gave them each fifty dollars in cash. They walked to the parking lot, and Drew thought, *First I get to see Callie, then I get a playoff game, and I get fifty bucks. This is awesome!*

As they drove away, Drew remembered that he was hungry.

Chapter 18
THE TEST

"I didn't want to say anything because I didn't want you to get nervous," said Jack.

"No worries," said Drew.

"Are you mad at me?"

"No. It's awesome. I'm just tired," said Drew.

"You did great, kid. The Commish was impressed," said Jack.

"It was hard to stay focused at the end of the game," Drew said.

"Don't worry about that. You didn't know that you had a game. If you had known, then you would have been more prepared," said Jack.

Jack pulled up in front of Drew's house, and Drew got his school bag and his ref gear from the trunk. The bag felt heavy. Drew leaned towards the driver's side window to say goodbye.

"I'll pick you up on Thursday night. Same time?" asked Jack.

"Great. Thanks. Any idea what rule we will learn about?" Drew asked.

"Keep studying Rule Seven about passing. Good luck on your English test tomorrow," said Jack.

"Thanks again, Jack. I can't wait for Sunday," said Drew.

"You've earned it. Say 'hi' to your Dad for me," said Jack.

"Will do." Drew went inside. His parents were cleaning up from dinner, but there was a plate waiting for him on the kitchen island. Drew sat on a stool and ate quickly.

"Whoa, slow down, Drew," said Mom.

"I feel like I haven't seen you all week. What's new?" asked Dad.

"I've been busy," Drew said.

Dad said, "Mom told me that you were studying at the library after school?"

"Yeah," said Drew. "Got a big English test tomorrow. It's on *The Odyssey*. Good story."

Dad gave Mom a startled look, "You read a whole book?" asked Dad.

"Yeah," said Drew.

"And you liked it?" asked Mom.

"Yeah," said Drew.

"And you studied for a test?" asked Dad.

"At the library?" said Mom.

"Yeah. So?" said Drew.

"Who are you, and what have you done with our son?" asked Dad.

"I also heard that he studied with Claire," said Mom.

"How did you know that?" asked Drew.

"Mrs. Murray texted me and offered to drive both of you home," said Mom. "She told me that Callie studied with you guys too." Mom and Dad looked at each other and smiled.

"Did you organize this little study group?" Dad asked.

"Yeah," said Drew.

"I'm impressed," said Mom.

"It's like your grandfather always told me: if you can't be smart, then date smart," said Dad, and he snuck up behind Mom and gave her a hug.

"Gross," said Drew. He changed the topic. "The Commissioner offered me a playoff game on Sunday."

177

"He did? That's great!" said Dad.

"So the game went well today?" asked Mom.

"Yes, and I earned fifty bucks," said Drew.

"Nice," said Dad.

Drew looked his Dad in the eyes and asked, "Did you know that the Commissioner was going to be at the game today?"

Mom broke in and said, "Jack called me then I called Dad, and we talked it over. We figured that it was stressful enough to accept a last minute assignment, so we kept quiet. Should we have told you?" asked Mom.

Drew thought for a minute, and he said, "No. I'm glad that you didn't tell me. At Candidates' Class they always say, 'They're all big games. Prepare the same way for each one.' If I'm going to get good at reffing football, then that's what I've got to do," said Drew.

"That's what you've been doing all along," said Mom.

"You've had a great season, Drew. You're the youngest official in the E.M.A.F.O's history, and you got a playoff game in your first year," said Dad. "What I wonder is: do you think that you'll stick with it?"

"When I was at the JV game yesterday, and I saw Troy catch a touchdown pass, I was happy for him. But I couldn't help comparing myself to Hingham's JV quarterback. I'm faster, and I have a better arm. There's still a part of me that thinks that I should be out there throwing touchdown passes to Troy."

"You were a good friend to support him. I understand that it must have been hard for you to watch instead of play," said Mom.

"Troy will get recruited, and I could have been recruited too," said Drew. "We could have been a two-for-one deal for the colleges: take the quarterback and his favorite target. We could have been roommates and best friends when we were old, just like Dad and Jack," said Drew.

"Who are you calling old?" asked Dad. "I wish that you had never been hurt too, but take it easy, Drew. If you stop and think about it, you're still chasing your dream: you're still friends with Troy, and you're still going to college. You know, Drew, playing college football taught me an important lesson about college admissions."

"What?" Drew asked.

"A lot of people think that sports is key, but if you really want to go to college and be successful there, then the way is pretty simple," said Dad.

"Yeah?" said Drew.

"Pick up a book, and read it," said Dad. "It's not as glamorous as a sports scholarship, but it's far more effective."

"And go to school every day, and do your homework," Mom added. "I agree with Dad. You did everything right today."

"I'm sorry that I keep bringing this stuff up," said Drew. "I don't want to be a crybaby."

"You're not," said Mom. "You're tough and hard working and stinky. Hit the showers, young man," Mom said. She hugged him, and Dad hugged him.

Drew went upstairs. After his shower, he checked his phone. There was a text from Claire, "Thanks for studying with us. I hope that your game went well." It was a group text. Drew didn't recognize the other number. *It has to be Callie's! Claire, you're the best!*

Drew wrote back, "Thanks again, guys. Game went well. See you soon!" Then he added Callie's number to his contact list. Drew lay on his bed and waited for them to respond, but he fell asleep.

Drew woke up the next morning and got ready for school. He checked his phone, but there were no texts. During breakfast he read over the pass interference rules. He tested himself by reading the example plays in the back of the rulebook. Drew was surprised by one of the plays that he read about: a receiver and a defender are running down the field. The quarterback throws the ball. Both players are running side by side looking back at the ball. Their legs get tangled, and they both fall down. According to Rule Seven, this is a legal play. The defender did not break the rules and try to intentionally stop the receiver from catching the ball. *Good luck explaining that one to an angry coach,* thought Drew.

Drew's school day revolved around the English test. During study hall, he finished his History homework and went over his English notes. On his phone he opened the picture of the library white board. He tried to memorize it. The bell rang, and he walked to Mrs. Fitzgerald's room. When he arrived, the tests were already face down on the desks. *Mrs. Fitz does not mess around,* Drew thought. *Am I nervous for an English test? I'm such a nerd!*

Mrs. Fitzgerald greeted the class and gave them directions. As soon as she was finished, Drew got to work. The first part was easy: matching characters' names to their descriptions. The next section was True/ False, and it was all about the plot. Drew cruised through the section to the multiple choice questions. He slowed at, "The Ancient Greek word for arrogance is_____" His choices were a) arête b) hubris c) ate D) Golden Mean. *I've never heard of 'Golden Mean.' That's out. 'Arete' is excellence. Is it 'hubris,' or 'ate'?* Drew tried to remember the answer and failed. His mind started to wander, but he caught himself. *I've got to get to the essay. My parents always say, 'When in doubt, pick C.'* Drew filled in the answer and moved on.

He quickly finished the rest of the multiple choice questions and moved on to the reading section. Mrs. Fitzgerald had photocopied two pages from Book 23 of *The Odyssey* onto the test, and she asked five multiple choice questions about them. Drew started to read, and his palms started to sweat. His stomach began to tighten. *We didn't read this part.* He took a breath and tried to think. *What do I look for? There are no study guide questions. Wait— there are test questions. I can read those first, and I'll know what to look for when I read.* Drew felt calmer, and he read the questions. *A question about plot, two questions about characters' motivations, a question about a Homeric Simile, and a question about theme. Got it.* Drew got to work on the reading. He read until he found the answer to a question, he answered it, and he continued reading. *Eat the elephant one bite at a time,* he thought. The task went by quickly, and Drew felt confident and sharp.

He got to the last section of the test, the essay. The prompt read, "Compare and Contrast two decisions that Odysseus made in the epic poem and explain what the decisions teach readers about leadership." *We were right! The essay is about leadership,* thought Drew. He took time to plan out his response, and he wrote his outline underneath the prompt:

Decision #1: Odysseus Trash Talks the Cyclops after he and his men escape.
- Odysseus is NOT a good teammate.
- His men try to keep him quiet, but he won't listen.
- He nearly gets everyone killed.
- Odysseus is arrogant. Why does he need to trash talk?

Decision #2: Odysseus decides not to tell his men about Scylla and tries to fight the monster himself.
- Odysseus is not a good teammate AGAIN!
- He worries that his men would get too scared if they knew the truth, but they have fought with him for years.
- A good teammate would have told the men about the danger and worked with them

The Decisions are the SAME: Odysseus is arrogant.

Lesson About Leadership: a great leader should be humble!

Drew stopped, and he raised his hand. Mrs. Fitzgerald was walking the rows, and she came to his desk.

"Mrs. Fitz, I made my outline, but I keep saying that the decisions are the same. Is that ok? Do I have to find a way that they are different too?"

"You don't have to do both, Drew. You decide. You're doing great. Keep going," said Mrs. Fitzgerald.

Drew drafted the essay. With a good outline he was able to write quickly. He read over his work and passed the test in with five minutes to spare. He knew he had done well.

When the test was over, Drew walked down the hall with Claire who had also finished early.

"How did it go?" she asked.

"We pretty much guessed the essay question. I'm glad that I studied with you guys. What did you think?" said Drew.

"Not bad. I'm glad that it's over because I didn't really like the book that much. I'm excited to start Shakespeare," said Claire.

"Me too!" Callie broke in from just behind them.

"Hey!" said Drew. *That sounded too excited.*

"Hey, Callie," said Claire.

"I stayed a little longer to read over my essay again. We almost guessed the essay. You guys must be good luck. I'll have to study with you again," said Callie.

"Cool," said Drew.

Claire looked at him and smirked.

"What was the answer for the one about arrogance?" asked Drew.

"Hubris," said Claire.

"Oops," said Drew. "Oh well. I still think that I did ok. Thanks, guys."

"See you later," said Callie.

"Bye, Drew," said Claire.

It was raining out, and gym class was inside. Drew decided to use the weight room instead of play volleyball. Drew warmed up with the class. In the weight room he did three sets of ten repetitions for bench press, seated rows, squats, and leg curls. *I hate leg curls,* he thought. His father always said that in college the coaches paid close attention to hamstring injuries. A hamstring injury told them who did the off-season workouts and who didn't. While he rested in-between sets, he thought about Callie. *She said I was good luck! Maybe she doesn't care that I'm not a QB anymore. Maybe she likes me. Maybe she just wants to be friends.* The uncertainty made Drew anxious, and he was glad that he could work with weights so that he could calm his mind. *There's only one way to know for sure,* he thought.

Drew knew what he had to do next.

Chapter 19
MEETINGS

On Thursday Drew was back in study hall. He looked out the window at the courtyard. That was all any student could do because students were not allowed to go in the courtyard. *What am I going to do: repel up the walls and escape?* Drew thought. It was cloudy. The foliage on the tree outside the window was thin, but the leaves were still striking shades of red. Drew refocused on his English homework. He had to put the verses of Sonnet 18 into his own words and answer some analytical questions on the back of the worksheet. He read, "Shall I compare thee to a summer's day." He wrote in the margins of his paper, "Are you like summer?" *I bet Callie loves this stuff, so I better look like I know what I'm talking about,* he thought. When he got to the line, "Rough winds do shake the darling buds of May," Drew thought about flowers. Before he left for school, he had taken one of his mother's flowers. She had arranged a beautiful bouquet of pale orange roses on the dining room table. The petals were pink at the tips. It was a big arrangement in a tall, narrow vase, and Drew was confident that his mom wouldn't miss one. He would have asked his mom for permission, but he didn't want to answer awkward questions. Drew couldn't walk around all day with a rose, so he cut the stem and stored it in a Tupperware container. He hid the container at the bottom of his school bag. He would not need the rose until the end of the day.

Drew finished with the sonnet just as the period ended. When he got to English, Mrs. Fitzgerald surprised the class with their graded *Odyssey* tests. *How can she read all of those essays so fast?* Drew wondered. Mrs. Fitzgerald built suspense by first handing out students' writing portfolios. She finally returned the tests. When his name was called, Drew walked up to the teacher's desk. The papers were folded in half, and Drew could not see the score. He looked at Mrs. Fitzgerald to try to catch a hint about how he had done. *Her poker face is good,* thought Drew. As he walked back to his seat, Drew resisted the temptation to look at his paper. He had learned that if he waited until he sat down, then he avoided some of his classmates' annoying questions, "What did you get?" Drew unfolded the paper and saw "95" at the top. Underneath his score Mrs. Fitzgerald had written, "Excellent effort, Drew!" Drew smiled, exhaled and leaned back in his chair. *Nailed it!* he thought.

Mrs. Fitzgerald finished passing out the exams and gave the class feedback on their work, "You worked very hard in class and on your homework, and it showed on the test. The class average was a 91, A-. I am very proud of you, and you should be very proud of yourselves." She began reviewing the matching, true/false, and multiple choice questions that the students had struggled with. A few students asked questions, but Drew kept quiet.

Next, Mrs. Fitzgerald made "Notes to Writers" about students' performances on the essay. Drew listened and looked at the comments that she had written on his paper. His supporting details and analysis were good, but his thesis statement was vague. His concluding sentence was specific. Mrs. Fitzgerald had circled this passage and written in purple ink, "Please add this to your thesis!" *No big deal. I can fix that,* thought Drew.

When Mrs. Fitzgerald finished giving her feedback to the class, she showed them an anchor paper that she had typed up. It was from someone in their class, but Mrs. Fitzgerald had omitted the name. Students took turns reading the essay aloud, and then the class discussed its strengths and weaknesses. When it came time to discuss how to improve the paper, the students made a few comments about grammar and word choice, but mostly there was silence. Finally, Mrs. Fitzgerald said, "Why is it so quiet?"

Scott answered, "Because the paper is so good that there is not much to say about how to make it better?"

"Good answer," said Mrs. Fitzgerald. "This paper was outstanding. I want to thank the student who wrote it for helping me show the class what my feedback means. I also want her to know that she did an excellent job, and I am very proud of her."

It's Claire, thought Drew. Finally, the class wrote down their strengths and weaknesses in their writing portfolios and brought them to the green filing cabinet by the closet. Mrs. Fitzgerald collected them and locked them up. After reviewing the test, the class began to share their summaries of Sonnet 18. When the bell rang, they had not gotten very far in the poem. Mrs. Fitzgerald had just enough time to remind them of their homework assignment before they were out the door.

Drew couldn't find Callie in the crowd, but he caught up to Claire, "That essay was yours wasn't it?"

"No," she said.

"You're kidding, right?" said Drew.

"No," she said.

"Do you know who wrote it?" Drew asked.

"I have an idea," Claire said.

"Who? Is it Callie's?" asked Drew.

"She and I always read each other's essays before we turn them in. It sounded like Callie," said Claire.

Drew rolled his eyes.

"Did you do ok?" she asked.

Normally, Drew kept his grades to himself, but not with Claire, "I got a 95!"

"Nailed it!" she said. They slapped five.

"Thanks again for studying with me," Drew said. "About that—what happened yesterday? When I asked Callie to go with me, she said she'd think about it, and then you both were standing at my locker. What happened?"

"She knows that we've known each other forever. She asked me to go," said Claire.

"Why? Am I on the highway to the friend zone?" asked Drew.

"Boys are clueless," said Claire. "She was nervous."

"Why? We were at a library. It wasn't like a date," said Drew.

"Don't let her hear you say that. She likes you, bonehead. She wants you to like her too. Gotta go to class," said Claire.

"See ya!" said Drew. He pumped his fist, and he smiled all the way to gym class.

In gym class Drew warmed up, and he ran three miles. *I will take tomorrow off so that I have fresh legs for the weekend.* Running usually calmed him down but not today. Drew kept thinking about seeing Callie again. When gym class was over, Drew rushed to the locker room. He changed quickly, and he reached into his bag to move the rose to the top. He didn't want anyone to see him. The bell rang, and Drew walked quickly. He stopped before he turned the corner near Callie's locker. He reached into his bag and took out the rose. His heart was pounding, but he kept going. There she was! Callie hadn't seen him yet. Claire's locker was nearby. She did see him.

"Callie?" said Drew.

Callie was startled.

"Sorry. Are you going to the Halloween Dance?"

"Maybe. Why?" she said.

Drew took a deep breath. He glanced at Claire, and Claire looked away. Drew said, "Do you want to go with me?" He handed her the rose.

"O my gosh. Thanks, Drew. Sure," Callie said.

"Great! I've gotta get home, but I'll see you tomorrow?" said Drew.

"See ya. Bye."

Drew walked away, and he didn't look back. His mind was racing. *That just happened! I just did that!*

Chapter 20

A LOVE POEM

On Thursday night after his Candidates' Class Drew asked his Dad, "Can I borrow one of the old shirts that you wear when you're working around the house?"

"No problem, Drew. What's up?" said his Dad.

"Halloween costume," Drew replied.

"And we get to see the final product before you go to bed?" asked Mom.

"Yes," said Drew.

"And you won't stay up too late working on the costume?" said Dad.

"No," said Drew. He went straight to his room. *They're so annoying*, he thought. Drew got to work. He found an old, gray pair of cargo pants that he used when he helped his Dad cut the lawn. Next, he went to his father's closet and found a faded, gray button-down shirt. He printed out an American flag and pinned it to his left shoulder. Next, Drew took a break and checked his phone. *Callie texted me!*

"The rose is so pretty. See you tomorrow! ☺" The message brought back some of the rush that Drew had felt that afternoon. He finished his costume and added his favorite pair of sunglasses and a name tag. He popped his collar for the finishing touch, and went downstairs.

"Maverick?" said Mom.

Drew nodded.

"*Top Gun*. A classic," said Dad.

"Get to bed," said Mom.

"Good night," said Drew.

"Good night," said his parents.

The atmosphere at school on Friday was electric. There were cool costumes everywhere. Scott was waiting at Drew's locker. He was also dressed like a fighter pilot.

"Maverick?" said Scott.

"Goose?" said Drew.

They laughed and slapped five. *I can't remember the last time that we laughed like that,* thought Drew. In English the class continued studying Shakespeare's Sonnet 18.

"The poem ends with 'So long as men can breathe and eyes can see/ So long lives this, and this gives life to thee.' Can anyone put the verses into his or her own words for us?" asked Mrs. Fitzgerald.

"Your beauty will live forever," said Claire.

"Good. Is that the only summary? Focus on the word *this*. It's an ambiguous pronoun. What if it stands for something other than beauty? What about the word *lines* that we talked about a few minutes ago?" said Mrs. Fitzgerald.

The class was silent for a few moments. Scott raised his hand. He still had his aviator sunglasses on. On Halloween the dress code went out the window. "He mentioned *lines* earlier in the poem, and he meant lines of poetry. Is he saying that the subject's beauty will live forever because he wrote about her?"

Mrs. Fitzgerald smiled, "Excellent work, Scott. Well done. What do you guys think of that?"

"That's pretty arrogant," said Callie.

Drew raised his hand, "When we read *To Kill a Mockingbird*, didn't Atticus teach us not to brag? But Shakespeare brags, and he was the greatest of all time. So which one is it?"

"Humility is a really important trait of successful people," said Mrs. Fitzgerald, "but there are exceptions to every rule. Can you think of any other exceptions?"

"Lebron James," said Scott.

"Donald Trump," said Claire.

"Kim Kardashian," said Callie.

"What does she even do?" asked Drew.

"You guys get it," said Mrs. Fitzgerald. Next, Mrs. Fitzgerald taught the students about scanning, the way to find the rhythm of a poem. She organized the class into pairs and asked them to scan the sonnet. They counted the syllables in each verse, paid attention to where their voices naturally rose and fell, and marked the rises with a "/" and the falls with a "u." Drew got paired with Claire. Her costume was Dr. Seuss's Thing Two. She had black yoga pants, a red t-shirt, a Dr. Seuss hat, and silly sunglasses. Drew stole a glance at Callie who was working on the other side of the room. She was dressed as Thing One. *She looks great no matter what*, thought Drew.

"Drew!" said Claire.

"Yeah. Sorry," said Drew.

"Stop staring," she said.

"Come on, I was—"

"Focus," she said.

"Alright. Alright. Take it easy," said Drew.

They finished their assignment quickly and chatted for a while. When the class was ready, Mrs. Fitzgerald asked certain groups to share their work. Each group shared one line of scanning. After four groups had presented, Mrs. Fitzgerald asked the class to search for patterns.

Claire saw it first. "The 'u' and the '/' are repeated," she said.

"Good. How many times?" asked Mrs. Fitzgerald.

Callie raised her hand, "There are ten sounds in each line. Ten divided by two is five. The pattern repeats five times!"

"Excellent, Callie. Now can you slow down your thinking and explain to the class how you got that answer?"

Callie said, "When we counted how many syllables were in each line, we found that there were ten. Then Claire found the 'you-slash' pattern, and it had two sounds. Ten divided by two is five."

"Thank you, Callie. Well done. That group of two beats has a name. It's called an *iamb*. When you are in your geometry class, what do you call a five-sided figure?" asked Mrs. Fitzgerald.

"A pentagon," said Drew.

"So you take the word *iamb*, and you make it an adjective, *iambic,* and you take the prefix *penta* and add it to *meter*, the poetry word for rhythm, and you get *iambic pentameter*. It's a famous rhythm in English poetry and in Shakespeare's poetry. What does it sound like?" asked Mrs. Fitzgerald.

"It sounds kinda like a horse," said Scott.

"Yes. Anything else?" asked Mrs. Fitzgerald.

"A heartbeat?" said Callie.

"Good," said Mrs. Fitzgerald. "And do you think that Shakespeare used the heartbeat rhythm on purpose in this sonnet?"

Claire raised her hand, "It makes sense because it's a love poem, and it sounds like a heartbeat."

"Exactly," said Mrs. Fitzgerald. She smiled and continued, "The music informs the meaning. And this isn't the only time that he does this. Just wait until Romeo and Juliet fall in love at first sight in Act One Scene Five!"

The class was almost over, and Mrs. Fitzgerald assigned the homework and wished the class a Happy Halloween. They packed their bags, and the bell rang. As the students filed out into the hallway, which was much crazier than usual, Mrs. Fitzgerald stood at the door handing out lollipops.

Chapter 21

THE HALLOWEEN DANCE

Drew's Mom and Dad drove Claire and him to the dance. His parents were going to meet Claire's parents for dinner on the harbor. The Murrays would pick up Drew and Claire after the dance. When they arrived at school, there was already a long line outside the gym. When Drew and Claire finally got inside, they were hit by a wall of hot air and sound. It was dark, and everyone was still in costume. Claire found her girlfriends, and Drew found Scott. The freshman team had returned from the Whitman-Hanson game an hour ago.

"I'm sorry about the game!" said Drew. It was loud, and Drew had to almost shout into Scott's ear.

Scott didn't say anything.

"What was the score?" asked Drew.

"28-14," said Brendan.

"How did the defense play?" asked Drew.

"We played pretty well, but we got tired and started missing tackles," said Scott.

"Yeah, the D couldn't get off of the field," said Brendan.

"How did you run the ball, B.?" asked Drew.

"Good at first, but I couldn't keep it going," said Brendan.

"After Brendan had a few good runs, they 'loaded the box' and used eight men to defend against the run," said Scott. "Without Troy it was hard to get the passing game going. If we had you and Troy, it wouldn't even have been close."

194

I don't think that compliment will ever stop being bitter-sweet, thought Drew. He took a breath and tried his best to move on. "Some things you don't have control over," he said. "It's frustrating. Believe me, I get it."

"True," said Brendan. Scott nodded his head.

"You guys know how good you are," said Drew. "Troy is starting on JV. At Thanksgiving you and Brendan will probably be called up to practice with the varsity. It's all going to work out. Next year the Panthers won't know what hit 'em."

Scott smiled. Brendan nodded his head. "Did you hear that Troy dressed for the varsity game tonight?"

"Whoa. Really?" asked Drew. He felt jealous anger flash behind his eyeballs, but he tried to mask it. *It's dark in here. Hopefully they didn't see that,* thought Drew. "Did he play?"

"I don't know," said Brendan. "He texted me that the team just got back. He should be here in a little while."

"He played really well this week against Silver Lake. I bet he got some playing time tonight," said Drew.

"We'll ask him on the dance floor. Let's go," said Scott.

"We'll follow your lead, Captain," said Drew. *Would I have played with the freshman today, or would I have dressed for the varsity?* thought Drew. *Have fun with your friends, and stop thinking about it.* He walked onto the dance floor, and he noticed Callie and Claire. *Let's go!*

Scott, Brendan, and Drew got out on the dance floor and started dancing with Callie and Claire. Pretty soon they were joined by the whole freshman team, and the dance floor was packed. Callie was smiling. Drew couldn't tell if she was laughing with him or at him, but he didn't care. At one point a big circle formed in the middle of the floor. Drew and Scott did their best Dab, the Caroline Panthers' touchdown dance. Their classmates cheered. The DJ changed the song, and the dancers took a break. Drew and Callie started talking.

"Thanks for studying with me the other day," said Drew, "I did pretty well on the test."

"You're welcome. Me too."

"Was it your essay that Mrs. Fitz read to the class?" Drew asked.

"Yes," said Callie.

"It was really good," said Drew. "If I can't be a good writer, then at least I was smart enough to study with one."

"When we have the *Romeo and Juliet* test, are you going to ask me to study with you again?" Callie asked.

"Yeah, of course," said Drew. He tried not to smile, but he couldn't help it, "Are you excited to read *Romeo and Juliet*?"

"Yes. What did you think of the sonnet?"

"It was hard to understand, but I liked it, I guess," said Drew.

"I've heard *Romeo and Juliet* is amazing," said Callie.

"I hope that it's not boring," said Drew.

Callie frowned.

Drew changed the subject, "How is coaching going?"

"Good. We have the playoffs this weekend. At least they're in Hingham. You're not going to be there are you?"

Drew smiled, "I am. Yesterday the Commissioner asked me to ref the fifth and sixth grade playoff game."

"So I get to see you again on Sunday?" Callie said.

"Yeah," said Drew. "Are you sure that you want to be seen talking to a guy in zebra stripes?"

Callie didn't hesitate, "Yeah. You're easier to talk to than you used to be."

"Ouch," said Drew. "What do you mean by that?"

"Put it this way: I wasn't sure if I liked talking to Drew the football star, but I like talking to you now," Callie said.

Drew smiled. The dance music started up again, and the dance floor started to fill up.

"Come on," Callie said, and she took his hand. They danced to "Just the Way You Are," by Bruno Mars, and "Something Just Like This," by The Chainsmokers and Coldplay. Drew was having so much fun dancing with Callie and his friends that he lost track of time. The dance floor seemed to get more and more crowded, and the gym was hot, but Drew didn't care. Finally, the DJ played a slow song, "Die a Happy Man," by Thomas Rhett. Drew danced with Callie. He looked around. Drew saw Claire dancing close by. She was dancing with Troy. *The varsity team must be back. I wonder how they did,* thought Drew. *Wait—Claire likes Troy? When did that happen? How come she didn't tell me? How come he didn't tell me?* Drew felt uneasy, but he refocused his attention on Callie.

When the music stopped, the DJ announced the final song. Troy was close by. Drew excused himself from Callie and asked, "Did you win?"

"35-28. We lost," he said.

"Sorry, man," said Drew.

"No worries. I got to play on Special Teams," said Troy.

Drew's first response was jealousy, and he was glad that the dance floor was dark. *Practice courage,* he told himself. He tried to be excited for his friend. "That's amazing! Congrats!" he said.

The final song began to play, "We Are Family." Drew and his friends danced, but Drew was tired and thirsty. When the song was over, the lights came on. In the confusion, Callie made her way over to Drew, "Thanks for dancing with me. I'll see you Sunday," she said. She kissed him on the cheek and walked away.

"Ohhhh!" said Scott and Troy.

Drew smiled, and they walked out of the gym.

Chapter 22

THE WARM-UP

On the ride home Claire did most of the talking with her parents. Drew's comments were limited to, "I'm glad that you had a nice time at dinner," "The dance was fun," and "Thank you for the ride."

When Drew got home, he texted Callie, "I had fun dancing with you. See you Sunday ☺"

Drew didn't have to wait long for a response, "☺"

As he lay in bed, his mind was racing, but he was tired. Drew soon fell asleep.

He woke up at 7:00 a.m. to the sound of his alarm. *Brutal! It's Saturday,* he thought. Then he remembered that he was reffing three Youth Football JV games in Cohasset. The games were an hour long, and they gave the players who did not start in the Sunday games a chance to learn and have fun.

Drew studied Rule Seven during breakfast, and his Mom drove him to the field.

"How was the dance?" she asked.

"It was fun. Did you have a nice time at dinner?" Drew asked.

"We always have fun with the Murrays, and the food is always good," she said. "Did you dance with Callie Walker?"

I'm glad that this is a short ride, thought Drew. "Yes," he said.

"Wasn't she a cheerleader last year?" asked Mom.

"She was," said Drew, "She's on the Dance Team this year."

"She's so cute," said Mom. "Did you kiss her?"

"Mom!" said Drew.

Mercifully, they arrived at Cohasset High School.

"Can you please pick me up at 11:30 a.m.?" asked Drew.

"Dad will pick you up," said Mom.

"Thank you, love you, bye!" said Drew.

Drew walked onto the field to meet his teammate. It was John, but he was wearing a knee brace.

"What happened? Are you alright?" Drew asked.

"Just old age. No big deal. I suppose I'll need a new knee one of these days, but I don't have to worry today, right?" John asked.

"Right," Drew said. "You're the brain, and I'll be the muscle." Drew had worked with John before, and he knew the drill, "I'll take the chains," said Drew.

"I love these games," said John. "We don't have to throw flags, and no one gets mad at us. There are a few parents who volunteered to help you with the chains," said John.

The game started. Drew focused on his mechanics and his pre-snap routines. *First down and ten yards to go. The ball is on the thirty-two. The line to gain is the forty-two. Three, three, three, two. The defense has eleven men.* Drew was also busy making sure the chain crew moved efficiently up and down the sideline. The chains were two poles covered by big, orange pads. They were connected by a chain that was ten yards long. The near pole was placed where the offense started their first play, and the far pole was ten yards away. The far pole marked the next first down. There was a third piece to chain crew, the down marker. It was a pole with a large rectangle on the top of it. The rectangle had big, orange numbers inside of it. The down marker, or "the box," told the teams what down it was, and its place moved as the offense moved. There were three parents who helped Drew work the chains. Drew marked with his foot the place where the box should go, and he was constantly looking over his shoulder to make sure that everything was where it was supposed to be and that the down marker showed the correct down. *I wouldn't want to miss a down. In the Candidates' Class we learned about the famous fifth down during the Colorado vs. Missouri game back in 1990. The refs forgot a down, and Colorado scored to win the game. Colorado went on to win a national championship.*

Running the chains was a lot to think about, but JV games were easy. John and Drew kept their flags in their pockets. If a player on the offense jumped before the rest of his teammates, John and Drew blew their whistles, "False start on the right guard, coach," Drew would say, and the coaches did the rest. The first two games went smoothly. The games were close; both teams scored, and the penalties were few and obvious to everyone. Drew was having fun, and he felt confident. It was a great warm-up for Sunday's playoff game, but during the third game Drew was tired.

The score was tied 6-6, and Scituate-Cohasset, who wear SciCoh on their royal blue and white jerseys, was driving for the go-ahead score. The SciCoh runner took a handoff into the middle of the line. Drew lost him in the crowd of players, but no one was moving very much so he raised his whistle to his mouth. Just as Drew was about to blow his whistle, the runner changed direction and ran for the far sideline. When Drew blew his whistle, the runner was breaking for open field. The players closest to Drew stopped dutifully and looked at him. The players around the ball kept playing, and the running back ran down the sideline towards the end zone. *Oh no! Oh no!* thought Drew. Drew froze. For a moment he stood staring at the players who had stopped. There was only one thing left to do, and Drew did it. He sprinted towards the ball carrier, and blew his whistle as loudly and as many times as he could.

Everyone stopped except Drew. He jogged straight to John.

"You didn't," said John.

Drew nodded his head and looked down at the ground.

"At least you didn't try to hide it," said John. He continued, "How?"

"When the ball carrier ran into the line, I thought he was stopped," said Drew. He looked at the ground again.

"When teams run the ball a lot, be slow with your whistle. It's better to make no sound at all than it is to blow an inadvertent whistle," said John, "What are you going to tell the Coach?"

Practice courage, Drew thought. "The truth," said Drew.

"Do you know the rules about inadvertent whistles?" asked John.

"Do over?" said Drew.

"When was the last time you read Rule Four, the rule about how plays start and stop?"

"It was sometime in September," said Drew. "It was one of the first rules that we went over in class."

"The coach has a choice: he can take a do over, or he can take the result of the play," said John.

"You mean a touchdown?" asked Drew.

"No. The touchdown would have happened because you blew your whistle, and most of the players stopped playing. What I mean is that the coach can have the ball where it was when you blew the whistle," said John.

"Hey, what's the hold up?" shouted the SciCoh coach.

Drew tried to remember, "He was a couple yards downfield. Maybe five," said Drew.

"Good," said John, "What was it? Second and six at the twenty-three yard line?"

Drew looked back at the chain crew. *Thank God they haven't moved!* he thought. The box showed a big, orange two on it, and it was positioned a little less than half way between the stakes. "Yeah, said Drew. It was second down. It looks like SciCoh needed six yards to get a first down."

"Go and tell the Coach what happened, and tell him that he can have third and one or replay the down," said John.

"Got it," Drew started to move towards the SciCoh bench then he said, "John, it might not matter, right?"

"I don't know, kid," he replied.

Drew walked past John towards the SciCoh Coach, "Coach, it was an inadvertent whistle. It's my fault. I'm sorry. Do you—" The Coach cut him off.

"It was a touchdown! Come on!" said the Coach.

"I'm sorry, Coach. It was my fault,"

"That's ridiculous, ref! You're gonna cost these kids the game! They deserve a good game too!"

"Alright, Coach, that's enough," said John. He stood beside Drew.

"Coach, you can have the ball where it was when the whistle blew, third and one, or we can replay the down," said Drew.

"Third and one," said the Coach.

John and Drew walked back to their positions, "Good work, kid," said John. "Now shake it off. Next play."

"Next play," repeated Drew. His mind was spinning. He reset the box, and the dad holding it asked, "What happened?"

"I made the worst mistake that a referee can make," said Drew. He turned towards the players and began his pre-snap routine, *Third and one on the eighteen yard line. The line to gain is the seventeen. Three, three, three, two.* The ritual calmed him a little, but his focus was gone. Three plays later SciCoh scored, and Drew felt like he could finally breathe again. The game ended in a 12-6 SciCoh victory.

As he and John walked off the field, the SciCoh Coach said, "Good game, refs!"

"You dodged a bullet," said John.

"Yeah," said Drew.

"Relax. It didn't affect the outcome," said John. "You don't ever want to make that mistake, but if you do, then these types of games are the perfect place to do it. Everyone is here to learn."

"It was a rookie mistake. It's the day before the playoffs. I should know better," said Drew.

"Inadvertent whistles happen to every official at some time or another," said John.

"Maybe I'm just not ready to ref a big game," said Drew.

"Hold on a minute," said John. "You've trained hard, studied hard, and worked hard. You've earned that playoff game, and you're going to do a great job. You got a big mistake out of your system today, and you learned that no whistle or a slow whistle is better than an inadvertent one. Thank goodness you learned that lesson before the playoffs and not during them."

"Good point," said Drew.

"Be confident, kid. You've earned that assignment, and you're ready for it," said John.

"Thanks, John," said Drew.

"Thank you. Like I always say, 'Your speed is going to keep me in officiating for a few more years.'"

"See you soon. And thanks," said Drew.

"Bye, Drew. Good luck tomorrow," said John. He waved and walked to his car.

Chapter 23
A GREAT CALL

Drew was grateful to see his Dad waiting for him in the parking lot.

"How did it go?" he asked.

Drew was silent.

"That bad, huh?" said Dad.

When they had turned onto Route 3A, Drew told his Dad the story.

"You got that out of your system before the playoff game, and you learned some good lessons. Relax. You'll be great tomorrow, and I have calzone," he said.

Drew ate a lot then he showered and took a nap. When he woke up, he felt better. He texted Scott, "Come over and watch football."

Scott texted back, "I'm in. Can Troy come too?"

"See you guys at 5 p.m.," texted Drew. Less than one minute later Drew got a text from Claire, "You, Scott, and Troy should come to my house and watch a movie." *I'm being used. Great. Fun night,* thought Drew. Drew wanted to watch football, eat, and hang out with the guys, just like they used to when he was the quarterback. He was annoyed at the change in plans, and he was annoyed about Troy liking Claire. *Why do I care?* he thought.

Drew wasn't annoyed for long, however. He received another text from Claire, "Callie's coming over too."

Drew texted Troy and Scott about the change in plans, and he texted Claire to let her know that they were coming. *Now I actually have to get ready for the night,* thought Drew.

Troy and Scott were a little late. They hung out at Drew's house for a while, and then they walked over to Claire's. The boys greeted Claire's parents, thanked them for pizza, and ate fast. They went to the living room to watch a movie. Drew sat next to Callie, and Claire sat next to Troy. Callie wore her hair down, and Drew noticed that she had lip gloss on. *Should I hold her hand?* Drew looked over to see if Callie's hand was anywhere near his. It was. Drew reached for Callie's hand. He held it, and she leaned on his shoulder.

When the movie was over, they all walked back to Drew's house. Drew and Callie walked behind the others. They cut through the tall oak trees in Drew's front yard. It was dark under the trees. Suddenly Callie grabbed Drew's hand and kissed him on the lips.

Drew held both of her hands. He said, "It was great to see you. I had fun."

"Me too," she said, "I'll see you tomorrow?"

"Yeah," Drew said. He thought of the playoff game, and he felt nervous for a moment, but Drew was still holding Callie's hands, and the playoff game felt far away.

"Goodnight," said Callie.

"Drew! Callie! Did you guys get lost?" said Troy.

Callie and Drew smiled. "Goodnight," said Drew, and he walked into the light of the front door. After the girls went home, Troy, Scott and Drew watched football.

"Did you kiss her?" asked Troy.

"Yeah," said Drew. His cheeks turned red.

"Ohhhh!" said Scott and Troy.

"Troy got a good night kiss too," said Scott.

Drew was a little annoyed, but he tried hard not to be, "When did all of that happen?" he asked.

"I don't know. At the dance, I guess," said Troy. "I've always thought that she was cute."

After Scott and Troy left, Drew went to bed. He sent Callie a text, "Good night," was all he could think of to say.

Callie's response was, "Good night."

That was quick, thought Drew. He was too excited to sleep. First he thought about Troy and Claire. *They are two of my closest friends. Shouldn't I be happy for them? Am I annoyed because they didn't tell me?* Drew paused and thought about their perspectives. *Troy's life is busier than it's ever been. I'm surprised that he has time to sleep. We're not together at practice every day like we used to be.* For a moment Drew felt sad, and he missed the camaraderie of the football team. *You were just hanging out with them an hour ago. Get it together, Drew.*

Next, Drew thought about Claire. *Troy has always been impulsive but not Claire. Claire would have planned a night like this two weeks in advance. We studied for the test together this week, and she's my partner in English class. Why didn't she tell me that she liked Troy?* Then the thought came to him: *Maybe the movie wasn't Claire's idea. Maybe it was Callie's, and Claire was helping her out.* Drew's mind continued to race. A lot had happened this week: the date at the library, the dance, the movie date. The insecurities that Drew had felt three days ago were long gone. *Callie doesn't care if I'm a quarterback or a ref. She kissed me. She likes me.* Drew gazed up into the darkness and smiled. He tried to stop his mind from racing. *I've got a big game tomorrow. Come on! Fall asleep!* Somehow, he had no idea when, he finally fell asleep.

Chapter 24
THE PLAYOFF GAME

Drew's dad woke him, "Come downstairs, and have breakfast. You've got church in an hour." Drew's body, especially his head, felt like they were made of stone. He forced himself out of bed, and he dressed and brought his rulebook downstairs. Drew studied as he ate. On this particular morning Drew liked how calm and peaceful it was at the Old Ship Church. *Church isn't so bad today*, he thought. It took his mind off of the game.

The nerves started as he left Old Ship. Drew's stomach felt tight, and his hands started to sweat. Every once in a while it felt like he had to catch his breath. He tried to eat again when he got home. He ate chicken soup and a banana, and he re-read Rule Seven. When lunch was over, he went upstairs and changed into his referee gear. He brought his bag downstairs, and he stretched on the living room rug. *Stretching at the field would be way too embarrassing*, he thought. Drew also did some dynamic stretches in his backyard. When he was done, his Dad drove him to Hingham High School, the site of the playoff game.

Drew and his Dad didn't talk on the car ride. *He gets me*, thought Drew. When they arrived, Drew's Dad said, "You're going to be great. Good luck. Have fun."

"Thanks, Dad. Love you," said Drew.

"Love you too, pal," he said.

Drew walked into the stadium, and he smelled the grill from the concessions stand. He heard the whistles from the referees and the cheers from the fans. *This reminds me of the Super Bowl game last year.* Drew looked down at his chest, but he saw black and white stripes instead of a game jersey. *Weird,* he thought. Drew walked through the gate and onto the field. Jack and the other officials were already there. Each introduced himself to the others. The previous game was ending, and the Hingham team was lined up under the goalposts. Their opponents, Silver Lake, were lined up under the goalposts on the opposite side of the field. Jack quickly reminded the officials of their assignments, "Drew, you're the Head Linesman today. You are responsible for the chains. There's a crew over there waiting for you. Did you bring your chain clip?"

Drew reached into his pocket and took out what looked like a braided, orange key chain. It was unusual because counting by fives it had the numbers between 5 and 50 on it. There was a little metal clip at one end, and a black, plastic square that could slide up and down the thing.

"Good," said Jack, "We've gotta head out to midfield for the coin toss. Before we do, remember: 1) Keep the kids safe 2) Keep the game fair 3) If you think it's a penalty, then it's not. Throw a flag when you know it's a penalty 4) Communicate. If you have a question, or if you think that we're doing something wrong, then let us know immediately. Don't wait to talk about it at halftime. It'll be too late. 5) Hustle, but don't hurry. We make mistakes when we rush. Whatever we do, let's make sure that we get it right. Now bring it in." The officials put their hands in the center. Jack said, "Let's work hard and have some fun out there. Let's go!" They broke their huddle and took their places.

The players were waiting on their sidelines. Jack called the captains into the center of the field for the coin toss. Hingham won the toss and elected to receive the kickoff. Drew stood at the fifty-yard line. He counted the receiving team and made sure that they were lined up according to the rules. When he had finished his inspection, he said to the blockers on the front line, "Wait for the referee's whistle. Good luck. You've worked hard to get here. Enjoy it," said Drew.

"Thank you, Ref," said the player in front of Drew.

Drew turned around and faced the Umpire. The Umpire gave the ball to the kicker, and the kicker placed it on the kicking tee. Drew raised his right arm and made a thumbs up.

The Umpire mirrored Drew's signal, and he said to the kicker, "Wait for the referee's whistle." In unison, Drew and the Umpire turned and jogged to their opposite sidelines. Drew took his place on the Silver Lake sideline, and he raised his hand to signal to Jack that he was ready. Jack blew his whistle to start the game.

Drew's heart was pounding. He took a deep breath, and he thought, *I wonder if Callie can see me?* Then he thought, *Focus, Drew!*

Silver Lake kicked the ball, and Drew's training took over. He jogged downfield to cover the kick, and his eyes focused on the blocking in front of the runner. The Hingham ball carrier ran to the other side of the field, and after he was tackled, Drew mirrored the Line Judge to show the spot where the next play would begin. The Hingham offense prepared to run its first play, and Drew worked with the chain crew to set up. Hingham used four receivers and wide formations. As the defense spread out, Hingham handed off to a quick running back who could find gaps in the Silver Lake line. Hingham chewed up yardage. Drew was very busy moving the chain crew. He also had to "set the clip." Its purpose was to mark the solid yard line nearest where the series began. If the chain crew were displaced, then Drew could use the clip to get them reset. Also, if the officials had to make a measurement to figure out if the offense made a first down, then they used the clip as the starting point.

Drew was nervous, and he was very busy. He was struggling to settle down and get into a rhythm. He barely had time to finish his pre-snap routines. On the fourth play of the drive, Hingham broke a long run down Drew's sideline. Drew turned and ran. He quickly closed the distance between him and the ball carrier. In his excitement, Drew nearly went stride for stride with the running back, *Slow down! You need to see the whole play!* he thought. Drew decelerated, and he let runner and the defender get ahead of him. He could see everything clearly. The runner distanced himself from the defenders and crossed the goal line. A few steps behind him, Drew stopped at the goal line pylon and raised both arms. The crowd roared.

"Great play! Great Play! I'll take your football, please," Drew said to the running back. The running back's eyes were wide with excitement, and he smiled at Drew. The two-point conversion was good, and Hingham lead 8-0. Drew jogged to the next kickoff, and he thought about the boy who had scored the touchdown. *That kid reminds me of me,* he thought. *When I scored a touchdown in the Super Bowl last year, it was one of the best feelings of my life. I've got to pay it forward.* Drew's breathing was deep and regular, like he had found his pace during a training run. He stopped at midfield. Before he helped the Silver Lake players line up for the next kickoff, Drew took a look around. The stadium lights had just turned on, and the trees beyond the stadium were dark gray shadows. Inside the bubble of the stadium lights, waves of sound and sight crashed down on Drew from the stands. He could still smell the smoke from the barbe-que. It was enough to overwhelm the senses, but Drew felt calm and confident. Every muscle in his body felt relaxed and strong, ready to spring into action at any moment. Drew smiled. *This is where I'm supposed to be,* he thought.

Hingham kicked off, and Silver Lake began their drive to the end zone. It was steady, and Drew got into a rhythm. When the first quarter ended, Silver Lake was within striking distance of a tying score. Drew led the chain crew to the other end of the field. When they were set, he gathered with the other officials around Jack, "You wing guys, remember: when we get inside the five, your first step is to the goal line," said Jack.

The second quarter started, and Silver Lake earned first down and goal to go at Hingham's eight-yard line. Hingham's defense stiffened. Twice Silver Lake ran into the middle of the Hingham line for short gains. On third and goal Silver Lake tried to run outside, but Hingham's outside linebacker made a great open field tackle at the two-yard line. Silver Lake called timeout.

"Get to the pylon," Jack told Drew.

After the timeout, Silver Lake lined up and ran the ball up the middle. *Get to the pylon!* Drew told himself. He kept his eyes glued on the ball carrier, and he shuffled to the pylon. Drew made sure that he was about three yards off of the sideline. Just before the runner was grasped by a swarm of Hingham defend-ers, he bounced the play outside and ran straight at Drew. One Hingham defender pursued. The play was a foot race to the cor-ner of the end zone. The running back was three steps from the goal line when the defender dove at his legs. The running back leapt and extended both arms. He hit the pylon with the ball, landed out of bounds, and slid past Drew, missing him by a foot.

Drew watched him land and thought, *The pylon is out of bounds IN the end zone. The ball is IN the end zone. Touchdown!* Drew raised his hands and blew his whistle loudly. The Silver Lake side erupted in cheers. Drew brought the ball to Jack, and Jack said, "Excellent position and excellent call. Great job, Drew!"

Drew always tried to make the right calls so that the game could be decided by the players on the field. However, the playoff atmosphere intensified the satisfaction of a making a good call. Drew felt a rush like he used to when he threw touchdown passes to Troy and Brendan. Drew smiled, and he thought, *Maybe I could get good at this.* Silver Lake also made a two-point conversion, and the score was tied 8-8. It stayed that way until halftime.

Chapter 25
A GOOD "NO CALL"

The officials sat on the Hingham bench during halftime. The Hingham cheerleaders took their places for their halftime performance. Callie walked by with the cheer coaches. She waved and smiled at Drew. He waved and smiled back. Jack looked at Drew and smirked. Drew stifled a smile and looked away.

"Great first half," said Jack to the crew. "We're gonna have a close game. You did a great job with your spots in the first half. Keep it up. Those spots will be important in the second half. Hingham's going to kick off. As soon as the cheerleaders are done, let's find out what side Hingham wants to defend and get going."

For the first time all day Drew felt cold and sore. Halftime was short, and the second half began with Hingham's kickoff. Drew quickly regained his focus. He was managing the chain crew, completing his pre-snap routines, and having fun. *I'm watching a great game, and I've got the best seat in the house!* he thought. Silver Lake made another sustained and methodical drive. Halfway through the third quarter the Lakers had advanced all the way to the Hingham eighteen-yard line, first down and ten yards to go. They ran the ball off tackle and gained five yards. *Second and five at the thirteen, line to gain is the eight, three-three-three-two*, thought Drew as he completed his routine. Silver Lake ran a sweep and gained four more yards. On third down and one, the Laker quarterback tried to sneak the ball between the center and the guard. He was met by a wall of Hingham defenders. No gain.

215

Drew set the down marker, turned back towards the center of the field, and focused on the next play: *fourth down and one at the nine, line to gain is the eight, three-three-three-two, know the ball carrier*, thought Drew. Silver Lake broke the huddle and jogged to the line of scrimmage. The noise from the crowd surged, and Drew could hear cow bells. *Cow bells are for dairy farms, not for football games!* he thought. The ball was snapped, and Silver Lake ran off tackle to Drew's side. The running back did not get very far before he was swarmed by a pack of Hingham defenders. Drew could not see the ball, and he reacted. He sprinted toward the pile. As he neared it, he saw the running back lying on the ground with the football locked in his right arm. Drew stopped and stuck out his left foot to mark where the tip of the ball had stopped, "It looks close, Jack! It looks close," he shouted.

Jack ran up to Drew to look at the spot from Drew's vantage point. "Let's measure it," he said, and he signaled for the game clock to stop. Drew held his position until the Line Judge came to hold the football in place. Drew jogged to his chain crew. The clip was on the fifteen-yard line. Drew took it between his thumb and forefinger and said to the chain crew, "Alright. Let's go." He jogged straight across the field with the two parent volunteers who were holding the stakes. Drew stopped on the fifteen-yard line directly behind the ball. He took one knee and placed the clip on the back of the line. A parent handed her stake to the umpire.

"Pull it," said Jack. The umpire pulled the stake. The chain straightened, and Drew could feel a tug on the clip. He pushed it firmly into the turf. The umpire pulled the chain as far as it would go, and the nose of the football just peeked out from behind the stake. "First down!" said Jack, and he signaled.

The chain crew jogged off of the field, and Drew thought, *It feels good to get it right.* "Thanks," Drew said to the chain crew. "I only need the down marker now." As soon as the down marker was set just inside the eight-yard line and the down was changed from four to one, Jack blew his whistle to resume the game. Silver Lake scored on the next play and took the lead. After a failed two-point conversion attempt, the score was Lakers 14 and Harbormen 8.

Hingham returned the Silver Lake kickoff past midfield. They quickly gained three first downs, and the third quarter ended. Drew led the chain crew to the opposite side of the field. Three plays later, Hingham tied the score, 14-14. Hingham's two-point conversion also failed.

Silver Lake began their next drive. They steadily gained yards, and they took a lot of time off of the game clock. The Lakers were deep inside Hingham territory. Their running back took a handoff and ran into the line. Again he was met by a wall of Hingham defenders, and he ran for the sideline. The defense anticipated the move and followed close behind. As the running back tried to hold off one defender with a stiff arm, another punched the ball loose. *Fumble!* thought Drew, and he took the blue bean bag from his belt and dropped it in front of him. It marked the spot where the running back lost possession of the ball. A Hingham defender scooped up the ball and ran it all the way to the end zone. Drew followed the play closely, and he was on the goal line with the Line Judge. Together they signaled touchdown, and the Hingham fans roared. Hingham's extra point attempt was unsuccessful again, but they led 20-14.

Silver Lake returned the kickoff into Hingham territory. They earned a first down using three running plays, and they called timeout.

The officials huddled around Jack. "They are probably going to pass," he said. "The wings will cover the passes, and the umpire will help with the short stuff. I'll watch the quarterback. If the quarterback is under pressure, then I may not see what happens downfield. If there is a penalty, then remember to tell me: who, what, where, and when," he said.

Drew started his pre-snap routine. The crowd was the loudest they had been all game. Drew could hardly hear himself think through the stomping, cheering, and ringing of cowbells. *First and ten at the thirty-three, line to gain is the twenty-three, three-three-three-two. There is one minute twenty-seven seconds left in the game, and Silver Lake is behind by a touchdown. They're going to pass. It's what I would do.*

Silver Lake broke the huddle and took their places on the line of scrimmage. The quarterback took the snap and rolled out to Drew's side of the field. Drew began to shuffle. The quarterback threw the ball, and Drew ran. His eyes focused on the receiver and the defenders around him. The pass fell incomplete. Drew signaled and relayed the ball to Jack. It was second down and ten yards to go. Again Silver Lake tried to pass the ball. This time the quarterback rolled out away from Drew. Drew moved downfield slowly. When the quarterback released the ball, Drew ran. Although the play was far away, Drew could see it clearly. The ball was thrown high and short. The receiver stopped running, and he was surrounded by three defenders. They jumped to catch the ball. Miraculously, the receiver fell to the ground at the fifteen-yard line with the ball tucked tightly against his chest. Drew ran to the fifteen-yard line, cut ninety degrees and sprinted across the field. He mirrored the position of the other wing official. When the official close to the play waved his arms above his head in a crossing motion, Drew mirrored him. The game clock stopped. There were fifty-eight seconds left in the game, and Silver Lake had a first down. They ran the ball, gained five yards, and called timeout.

When the officials huddled around Jack in the middle of the field he said, "Silver Lake has one timeout left. Make sure the coaches know it."

After they broke the huddle, Silver Lake tried another run play. They were stopped 2 yards shy of the first down. The Lakers called their final timeout.

"Silver Lake is out of timeouts. Wings, they are going to take two shots at the end zone. If you read pass, then release. I want you to have great position to see the play in the end zone," said Jack.

The players returned to the field, huddled briefly, and took their places. The crowd noise was loud and unrelenting. Silver Lake snapped the ball, and the quarterback ran away from Drew's side. *They're trying the same play that worked last series*, thought Drew. The quarterback threw the ball, Drew drifted towards the end zone, and a half dozen players from both teams leapt for the ball. This time it fell to the turf. Drew helped relay the ball to Jack, and he checked the chain crew. *Fourth down and two from the seven-yard line. The line to gain is the five. Three-three-three-two. Silver Lake is going to throw to the end zone. This is it*, he thought.

The players broke the huddle, and the fans were louder than ever. *Breathe, Drew. You've got this*, he thought. The quarterback took the snap and rolled out to Drew's side. Drew shuffled towards the end zone keeping one eye on the receivers and the other on the quarterback. When the quarterback released the ball, Drew turned and ran. Drew could see the receiver closest to the sideline running stride for stride with a defender. Both were looking back for the football, and they were running towards the back corner of the end zone. Then they both fell down! The ball fell to the turf just beyond them. Drew slowed down, and he felt panic welling up inside him. *Was it interference?* Drew slowed to a walk. He put his hand on his belt like he was going to throw a penalty flag. *Wait, they were both looking up at the football, their legs got tangled, and they tripped and fell. No one tried to stop anybody from catching the ball. I read this example play in the rulebook. It's not interference. It's not an obvious attempt to stop an opponent from catching the ball. It's not interference!* Drew stopped near the players on the ground. He blew his whistle and signaled incomplete.

The fans on the Hingham side cheered, and the fans on the Silver Lake complained, "Come on, Ref. You've got a flag. Use it!"

"The kid's on the ground. How is that not pass interference?" shouted the Silver Lake coach.

Drew ran after the football, and he heard a loud whistle blow three times. Drew looked back to the center of the field, "The game is over!" Jack said. Drew jogged to Jack and gave him the ball. Jack held it above his head, the signal that the game was over. "Go get your chain clip, and thank your crew," he told Drew.

Drew retrieved his clip and thanked the crew. On his way back to the center of the field, the Silver Lake coach approached him, "How was that not a penalty?"

"It wasn't interference, Coach. They were looking back towards the ball, their legs got tangled, and they fell down. It's—"

"It's not a penalty, Coach," Jack was by Drew's side. "There was no 'obvious intent to impede.'"

"But my player was on the ground!" said the coach.

Jack took over, "I hear what you're telling me, Coach. Your receiver fell to the ground. He fell. The defender didn't put him there on purpose. There was no pass interference. Come on, Drew. Let's go."

The officials walked off of the field together.

"It was the right call, wasn't it Jack? Why is the coach so mad?" asked Drew.

"It was a great call, kid. Remember: he wants his team to win. You don't care who wins. Sometimes you and the coach are just not going to agree," said Jack. "People are passionate about football. We both were when we played. Don't let him bother you."

As they got to the gate, the Commissioner approached them. He said, "Excellent work, everyone. You gave the kids a great game. Drew, that was a good 'no call!'"

"Thank you, sir," said Drew.

"You're going to be great at this if you keep at it," said the Commissioner.

"Thank you," said Drew. He took a deep breath and smiled. He added, "I have a great mentor."

"Yes, you do. Don't forget to get paid." The Commissioner handed them all envelopes with fifty dollars in them.

"I'll see you at the Candidates' Final Exam?" asked the Commissioner.

"Yes, sir. Thanks again," said Drew.

Drew shook hands with his crewmates, and turned towards the parking lot. He had not gone two steps when he was stopped by a hug. It happened so quickly that he had no idea who it was.

"Hey!" By the voice he knew it was Callie. Claire was standing with her.

"Hi!" said Drew. "Are you sure you want to be seen hugging a referee?"

"You did well out there," a voice interrupted them. "I'm Mr. Walker, Callie's dad. Callie's younger brother plays on the team. You let the players decide the game. Thanks," he said.

Drew shook his hand, "It's nice to meet you, sir. Thank you."

"This is my mom," said Callie.

"Hello, Mrs. Walker. I'm Drew Hennings. Nice to meet you," he shook her hand.

"And I'm Drew's dad, Mike Hennings."

"Dad?" said Drew.

"You didn't think that I would miss your first playoff game as a referee did you? Great job on the pass play in the end zone. It was unlucky that the kids tripped, but it wasn't illegal. Good 'no call,' Drew," said Dad.

"I hear that the kids did well on their *Odyssey* test this week," said Mrs. Walker.

"Callie and Claire, thank you for being a good influence on my son. The smartest thing that he did was ask to study with you," said Dad.

Callie smiled, and Dad ignored the critical look that Drew gave him.

"Drew, I've got the Patriots' game recorded, and I need your help handing out Halloween candy. I can drive Claire home."

"See you at school tomorrow," said Callie. As they walked out of the stadium, Callie looked back at Drew and smiled.

A year earlier, in this very place, a significant part of Drew's life had ended. A long and challenging journey had brought him back here, and as Drew walked out of the stadium gate, he felt that a new and important part of his life was just beginning.

ABOUT THE AUTHOR

Dr. Struzziero played football and sang a cappella for Tufts University. He teaches English at Hingham High School; he officiates high school football with the Eastern Massachusetts Association of Interscholastic Football Officials, and he attends First Parish Church in Cohasset, MA where he lives with his wife and two daughters.